Fire C

Nathan Keonaona Chai

Palmyra Press

For my father,
Henry Keonaona Chai II,
who taught me how to live and how to die.
I miss you.

CHAPTER 1

The whole thing hinged on a meaningless detail: a fist-sized rock hidden by a weed. The first five Marines in the patrol, including staff sergeant Davison, missed it. Jason Chang never saw it, but his boot came down safely several inches away. Jason's best friend, Rodney Taylor, stepped over it. Next came Austen, and as though it had been set there just for him by someone who knew what was coming, his heel fell on the corner of the rock. Jason heard the pop and turned to see Austen on the ground, clutching his ankle, wincing in pain.

Five minutes later they were all sitting in the shade of an ancient stone wall, waiting for a Jeep to come pick up Austen and drive him back to base. Jason and Rodney sat at the end of the line, a little ways apart from the rest of the Marines. Nineteen years old with a strong lean build, Jason wore a pair of yellow sport sunglasses and two day's stubble. His features hinted at Asian ancestry, but his hair was light brown, almost blond.

"Hottest day of the century and we're stuck out here," Jason said, unlacing his boots and slumping back against the rugged stone. "What are the odds that rock would be right there?"

Rodney shrugged. A black man from Vegas, he was twenty-three years old, married, with two young girls. He had a friendly face, a big easy grin, bright eyes, strong chin—a face that made people like him even before they knew him. And Rodney, like Jason, was a talker, a man who had perfected the art of casual conversation. After their long months of patrols, they'd grown as close as brothers. But today Rodney was quiet and distant.

"What are the odds?" Jason repeated, glancing at Rodney, waiting for him to take the lead. But Rodney said nothing. Jason sighed, set his M-16 on the ground beside him, the muzzle facing an abandoned mud-brick building across the dirt road, took an MRE out of his pack, looked at it, but didn't open the plastic food packages. For three months he'd been working here in the Narang province of Afghanistan, about 100 miles northeast of Kabul. The mountains around the province were barren and dry—like huge gray rocks dropped onto the desert by careless design. The city of Narang itself, a haphazard collection of clay and brick buildings ground down by decades of war and poverty, had only one resource so far as Jason could tell: the poppy fields to the north, which were harvested and processed into opium. There had been no fighting here for months, nor any sign of Taliban holdovers, and Jason figured these patrols were a waste of time.

"I don't know if this is a good idea," Rodney said suddenly, studying his untouched food.

"What?" said Jason.

"This. Stopping here."

"Don't worry, Rod. It's too hot for fighting. I mean, if someone could figure out how to heat up every day like this, we'd finally have peace on earth. People would be too tired to fight."

As though he hadn't heard, Rodney continued to stare down at his food.

"You all right, buddy?" Jason asked.

Rodney nodded.

"Seriously, man, you don't have heat stroke or something do you?"

"I'm cool."

"Right," said Jason, shaking his head. "Cool."

He looked down the line of resting soldiers to staff sergeant Davison, who was scooping pork chow mein out of the small plastic case. "Hey, Daveys, what about we call off this war and go find us some air conditioning?"

Davison just smirked and pulled from his canteen. Jason slouched back against the wall again and stared out at the broken gray cityscape.

"I tell you what," he said to Rodney. "Whoever decided to settle here in the first place must've been kicked out of somewhere else. You know what I'm saying, bro?"

"Not a place I'd want to set up camp," Rodney said without energy.

Jason glanced at Rodney, trying again to measure out his mood, then he took out his applesauce, popped the tab, and started eating slowly, like it was a chore. A short way down the street, two gray dogs so gaunt Jason could count their ribs trotted from a bombed-out building and froze when they saw the soldiers. Davison raised his hand as though to throw a rock, and they hobbled away back into the rubble. On a small rise just past the dogs' territory, another soldier, Rawlins, had been assigned by Davison to be lookout. He stood lazily scanning the streets.

"Civilian car's coming!" he shouted. For Davison's sake, he added, "And guard duty in the sun still bites!"

Moments later, a dirty VW Bug with a shattered rear window rounded the corner and drove by, stirring the dust, belching out exhaust. Most of the soldiers picked up their weapons and eyed the driver as it passed, put them down again when it had gone. Then quiet and the inescapable heat.

Rodney looked at Jason and seemed about to say something, but instead he glanced back over his shoulder at the others, then slid up close.

"Hey, Chang, you mind if ask you something?" he said, almost whispering.

"Fire away."

"You believe in dreams?"

"Have em all the time."

"I'm serious, Chang."

In the distance, a car horn honked four times and then went quiet.

"What kind of dreams, Rod?"

Rodney leaned in close and spoke even quieter. "This is gonna sound crazy, you know, but I had this dream last night."

"Yeah?"

"Except it wasn't like any I had before."

"What happened?"

Rodney looked out at the city for a time.

"I was back home in Vegas with my girls and my wife." He paused, as if weighing his next words. "They said they was there to tell me goodbye."

Jason looked over at Rodney, who was staring down at his hands, fingering his unopened MRE. A hundred yards down the road, four bearded men stood watching from a dusty intersection. When Jason raised his eyes to meet theirs, they quickly moved on. Rodney didn't notice them.

"I wouldn't worry, bro," Jason said, still looking after the men. "Sometimes you just got to put that stuff out of your head."

"This wasn't no regular dream, Chang. I'm tellin you, it was like I was there, like I was sittin there at home. I could smell my wife's perfume. I could feel my daughters' tears. It was like I was really there."

Jason sat there, still holding his fruit cocktail, trying to think of something to say. Down the dirt road a short distance a woman veiled in a black burka turned the corner and started toward them, but when she saw the soldiers sitting there, she spun round and almost ran back the way she'd come. And then everything was still, no movement anywhere, almost like a ghost town. Beyond Jason could see heat waves rising off the desert. "You're starting to trip me out," he said at last.

"Tell me about it."

"So what happened after that?"

"That's all there was to it. But I can't shake it off."

"Don't sweat it, Rod. Hang with me for today and we'll lie low. Tomorrow's another day. Things'll look better tomorrow."

Rodney stuffed his MRE back into his pack. He didn't look convinced.

"You know what we should do?" Jason said. "Tonight we should go over to the offices and email your daughters. They get email, right?"

"Yeah. At the school library."

"Well there you go. That's what we'll do."

Rodney nodded. He took another long swig from his canteen and water dripped down his chin.

"Besides," Jason said, "nothing can happen to you. I'd never get through all these mindless patrols without you."

Rodney seemed not to have heard. He turned to Jason and said quietly, "Can I ask you a favor?"

"Of course."

"Say a prayer for me."

Jason stared back at Rodney, wondering if was serious.

"I'm serious, man. I'm really spooked."

Jason looked away. On the lookout hill, Rawlins was now sitting down, leaning back on his hands.

"Nobody's even fired a shot around here in months," Jason said.

"You're my best friend, Jason."

"I haven't prayed since I left Esperanza. You know that."

"Yeah, but you prayed when you lived in Esperanza, right?"

Jason nodded.

"And you still know how to pray, right?"

"I can't, Rod."

"I'm askin you as a friend."

Jason looked at the other soldiers, then back at Rodney. "I'm sorry but I just can't. And besides, you're way tighter with God than I am."

Rodney said nothing more, so they sat and watched as a hot breeze came in off the desert and spun sand over rocks and crumbling walls and through broken windows. Ten minutes later, Davison got a radio call and announced that Austen's ride was on its way and that it was time to get ready to move. Grumbling, the patrol loaded the leftovers into their packs. Jason was about to stand and stretch when he heard a voice. Soft but unmistakably clear, it seemed to come from inside his own head: *Don't stand up.*

He glanced at Rodney, who was squatting down on his pack, adjusting the straps on his helmet.

"What?" Jason said.

Rodney looked up at him.

"You didn't say anything?" asked Jason.

Rodney shook his head. "Now *you're* trippin."

Jason shook his head and he was about to stand again, but once more he heard the voice, forcefully now: *Don't stand up!* Confused, Jason slouched against the wall and looked down the line at the others. No one was standing yet. No one was looking his way. No one else had heard the voice.

"Let's get this over with," said Rodney.

Standing, he slung his pack onto his shoulders. Almost too quick to be heard, there came just above Jason a sudden hiss and a cracking, splattering sound. He looked up just in time to see Rodney fall, the weight of his pack pulling him back, his feet pinned beneath his butt, blood spattered across his shoulders and face. A split second later the crack of a single shot reached them.

"Everybody down!" screamed Davison. But before anyone else could stop him, Jason jumped forward and grabbed Rodney's shoulders, trying to find where he'd been hit.

Then he let go. The back of Rodney's head was missing.

The world began to spin around Jason, and everything seemed to blur into one incomprehensible event. He heard someone shouting something about a sniper, he was aware of someone, maybe himself, yelling over and over again for a medic, he tasted vomit, he saw the other soldiers crouched against the wall, their faces tight, he saw his own hands, stained red, clutching Rodney's shirt, he heard Davison screaming into his ear, something he couldn't understand . . . then the wall exploded in a furious pulse of sound and light.

Pain sliced through his left leg, the air was knocked from his lungs, and he was thrown to the ground. Davison crouched beside him, stunned, a hand to his chin, blood dripping through his fingers. He could hear nothing over the ringing in his ears. Jason's head lolled to one side and he found himself staring at Rodney's blood-spattered face, one side painted dirt-gray where it had hit the road, his dark eyes open and blind, his jaw slack and crooked. Before he could fully regain his senses, something heavy smashed against the side of his head, the world drained of color, and darkness took him.

CHAPTER 2

ou Coldwell sat on a blanket in back of his father's rust-flecked pickup, a road map of Utah spread open across his lap. He was fourteen years old, stick thin, with overlarge glasses, and hair cut in a crooked line across his brow. Buried in a sleeping bag beside him, his father, Paul, lay snoring. The pickup sat on the shoulder of a two-lane highway, where desert sage and mesas stretched away in all directions, almost as though the two of them were the only humans left in the world. Lou squinted down at the state map, scanned along the southern border until he found a dot labeled "Kanab." With his finger he traced a route from that starting point along a string of state highways until he came to another dot near the center of the state. Esperanza, so small and out-of-the-way you could easily miss it.

Lou had just begun trying to measure out the space between the two towns, using his thumb as a ruler, when in the distance along the line of black asphalt, a windshield glinted in the sun. Lou looked up. It was another pickup, painted sport-car red, large wheels, moving fast. He nudged his father. Paul didn't wake.

"I think Melvin's truck's comin."

He shook his father again, but Paul slept on. The truck, close now, braked hard, pulled off the highway, and skidded to a stop on the gravel. The slow grumble of the diesel quit, the door opened, and an old man with slate hair pulled back into a ponytail got out, the gravel crunching beneath his lizardskin boots.

"Mornin, Lou," he said.

Lou watched the new arrival as though he knew him to be a threat. The old man sauntered over, leaned on the truck bed, and looked down at Paul's sleeping bag.

"Still out, eh?" he said.

"We was up late."

"I bet you was."

The old man opened the tailgate and grabbed the closed end of Paul's sleeping bag. The polyester made a soft zipping sound as he pulled it across the bed. Paul and the sleeping bag slid over the tailgate and thumped onto the gravel below. For a second or two, the bag thrashed, then the zipper pulled back and Paul fought his way out of the tangled fabric.

He was a man of thick strong lines, his face dark, wide, and pockmarked, several pale scars standing out in his buzzed black hair. He stood barefoot, blinking in the sunlight, his mouth open. Then he saw Melvin and his expression instantly hardened.

"I got a call from Fay Blanchard," Melvin said, as though they'd been chatting. He sat down on the chrome bumper of his own truck. "She heard you packin last night. Naturally, I told her she must be mistaken, that there's no way you'd be dumb enough to fly the coop at a time like this."

"What'd you come out here for, Uncle Melvin?"

"Well, Fay just kept on insistin and since I had nothin better to do on a Monday morning, I figured I'd take a drive down the highway and see what all the fuss was."

Melvin stood again and walked around to the other side of truck. Several cardboard boxes lay stacked on the ground; a few had no tops and overflowed with clothes. One had been packed full of old boxing gloves and a speed bag. A rusty ten-speed leaned against the fender.

"Despite what Kent may claim," said Melvin, looking over the cargo, a smile flickering across his lips, "you are capable of hard work. You clear all those boxes out just to make room to sleep?"

"I asked what you wanted."

"I think you know full well what I want."

"I left the rent on the table."

"And what about the final arrangements? I don't want to be caught holdin the ball when time runs out."

Something in Melvin's words made Paul flinch. He stood there barefoot on the roadside, his face pained, his fingers clenching and relaxing. He turned suddenly to Lou.

"Get in the truck," he said.

"But I don't—"

"Just get in! There's some things I got to talk about alone out here."

Lou hesitated, looked at Paul, at Melvin. Then he jumped out of the truck bed, climbed into the passenger side, and slammed the door.

"Roll up the windows," Paul barked. He turned back to Melvin, and when he spoke his voice was quiet, but quivering with anger. "I haven't told him nothin about that yet so you best keep your mouth shut."

"Well you should've told him! Or are you still hoping that dead-beat Teresa will come to the rescue?"

Paul covered the distance to Melvin in three quick steps. Melvin opened his mouth, but before he could form a word, Paul's open hands hit his chest. Unable to keep his feet beneath him, Melvin fell backward, catching himself on his hand and elbow.

"More than once I told you," said Paul, his face flushed, "how I raise my son is not up to you."

"Just who do you think I am?" Melvin scrambled back to his feet, swatted a few bits of gravel from his elbow, and straightened his shirt and belt. "You think I'm just another idiot you can jerk around? You wouldn't even be here if not for me."

Paul turned away, walked to the boxes stacked beside the truck, and started hefting them into the back of his truck. "I'm goin to Esperanza," he said without looking at Melvin. For the first time in the conversation, Melvin looked surprised. Paul grabbed another box, and threw it into the truck.

"Why?" said Melvin, as though he could make no sense of it.

"We'll camp for a few weeks and get the house in living order. I start work at the copper mine end of June." Paul picked up the bike and swung it into the truck, then looked back at his uncle. "Our room at your motel is clean. You can start rentin it again today. No need to waste more money."

"This was never about the *money*," Melvin said.

Paul loaded the last box, threw up the tailgate, tossed in his sleeping bag, and put another box over it so it wouldn't blow out.

"Don't lose any sleep on our account," he said, then he walked to the cab and climbed in.

The engine started, revved, backfired. The wheels threw up a plume of gravel and dust, and the truck lurched onto the highway. For a time Melvin watched it go, watched it diminish to little more than a speck on the long ribbon of desert road, then he dusted off his hands, got into his own pickup, swung a U-turn, and drove away fast in the opposite direction.

■ ■ ■

The old pickup rattled down the desert highway. Lou sat with his arm in the open window and stared out at the broken mesas and the sagebrush and the blush of spring wildflowers. A few clouds had blown in and they cast wide rushing shadows over the desert. After a while, he lifted a backpack from the floor, unzipped it, and took out a bag of carrots.

"I saved these for you," he said.

Paul looked at the bag, then back at the road.

"Thanks, but not right now."

They drove for a time in silence. A semi whooshed by in the opposite lane, the wind shaking the pickup.

"Open up that glove box for me," said Paul.

"What for?"

"My aspirin's in there."

Lou opened the box and took out the pill bottle. "How many you want?"

"Four."

"I thought you was only supposed to take two."

"You my doctor now?"

"No."

Lou emptied four pills into his palm and passed them to Paul, who swallowed them two at a time without water.

"Another headache?" asked Lou.

Paul nodded.

"You been gettin a lot lately."

Paul looked straight ahead and said nothing. A moment later he slammed down the brakes, pulled the truck fishtailing into the field beside the road, threw open his door, and leaned out. Lou turned away. He knew from the sound that his father was vomiting. A few seconds later Paul sat up again, spit a few times, and shut the door.

"I think I got some bad meat last night," he said weakly, his face pale and drawn. Sweat beaded on his forehead.

"I ate the same as you," said Lou.

Paul shifted the truck into gear and steered it back onto the road. Sensing his son's eyes on him, he forced a weak smile and wiped his brow. "Glad to get that out of me. You know, I'm actually feelin pretty good now. Almost like I could go twelve rounds with "Ali."

When the concern didn't leave Lou's face, Paul glanced over and smiled again. "This ain't no way to drive. We got to have some music. What you got over there?"

"Same tapes as always."

"Well choose one."

"I don't care."

"All right. How about some James Taylor?"

Lou found the tape on the floor under his seat. Paul rolled down his window, turned up the volume, and the two of them hollered out the words to "Copperline" with Taylor and his band and the desert passed by outside. Soon they were laughing at each other's miserable voices and seemed to forget, or at least pretend to forget, all thoughts of Melvin and of Paul's headaches and nausea.

CHAPTER 3

*E*very second, without fail, the machine beeped, a high tone that worked its way down through the darkness. Jason couldn't see, couldn't move; his only sensation was the beeping. For a long time he lay there in the haze between waking and sleeping, until at last he felt a hint of pain in his left leg. Steadily the pain grew worse, turned from an ache to a raw throb. He opened his eyes.

He lay on his back in a long plain room with an unlit fluorescent tube directly over him, an IV bag at his side, and a thin blanket covering him. In the darkness he could just make out seven or eight other sleeping men. He had no sense of where he was, and he felt far too tired to try to remember.

A bleary-eyed man wearing scrubs entered the room and paced among the beds, his shoes squeaking on the polished concrete floor. He flashed a dim red light over the men's faces. When the light shone on Jason, he stopped.

"You're awake," he said dully.

"Where am I?"

"Military hospital in Kabul. They brought you in a few hours ago."

"What happened to me?"

"Your leg's all messed up. And you got conked on your dome."

Jason stared at the medic, tried to remember how this had happened. In a rush of images and sounds, it came back. The rifle shot, Rodney dropping, blood splattered over his face, confusion, explosion. And now here he was. He thought he should feel something, anything, but he didn't. Instead, he felt strangely insulated, as though his emotions hadn't awakened with his body.

"You should get some sleep," said the medic. "It's two in the morning."

"Don't think I can."

"The leg?"

Jason nodded. The medic walked to the end of the bed, picked up the clipboard that hung there on a thin chain, and shone his red light over the notes.

"I'll get you some more pain med," he said.

The medic left. Jason put his hands over his face and lay there, unmoving, his breathing shallow. When the medic came back into the room, Jason didn't open his eyes.

"This'll knock you out for the rest of the night," the medic said. He injected the painkiller into the IV line. It was then that Jason remembered the voice. But it was too late to think anything more—the world was hazing and drifting away and soon he was asleep once more.

■ ■ ■

The next day passed for Jason in a fog of medication, a twilight world of half-sleep. At times, when his mind cleared some, he thought about Rodney—how he'd attended the chaplain's Christian meetings in Narang every Sunday; how he'd read from his Bible every night; how he'd prayed and never cursed and spoken often about Jesus' love for all nations; how he'd even tried not to pass judgment after Jason admitted he no longer believed in God. How he'd known something bad was coming. And now he was dead. Jason could make no sense of it. It seemed unreal, a dream that would break with dawn.

In the early evening a doctor arrived and told Jason he was being sent to Ramstein Air Base in Germany, where he would undergo surgery and then fly home. A few minutes later Lieutenant Davison visited. Rough stitches traced an arc across his chin. He took off his hat and sat down on an empty bed. Most of the other injured men slept, although a few read paperbacks or out-of-date magazines shipped over from the States. In quiet voices they spoke of trivialities—sports and hobbies and things they missed. Jason told Davison about his hometown of Esperanza, Utah. A small mining town, he said. As boring as an algebra lesson.

They talked for a few minutes more, and although they laughed and acted happy to see one another, the conversation felt forced. At first Jason wanted to tell Davison about the voice, ask him what he made of it, but in the end he figured Davison would think he was crazy. When the time came for Davison to leave, he stood and put on his hat and sighed. "I got to tell you I'm sorry about what happened. I know how close you and Rodney were—"

"Listen, bro," Jason interrupted. "You don't owe me anything."

"Yes I do. I had command. We shouldn't have camped out there, and we both know it."

"You can't know everything. You're not God."

"You can get your apology from God later. For now, mine'll have to do."

Jason was startled by the words. He looked away and seemed to be thinking.

"You have a safe trip home," Davison said at last, and then he walked down the row between the cots and out of the room.

CHAPTER 4

*P*aul Coldwell slapped a "For Sale" sign on the back window of the old pickup and sat down on the open tailgate. The truck had been parked in the front yard of a small house with two boarded-up windows and a porch with cracked concrete steps and a splintered wood rail. To the side of the house stood a carport with a green corrugated plastic roof, which sagged under the weight of many seasons of blackened leaves. An old maple lived in the middle of the yard, half its limbs green, the others bare and dry. Colonies of waist-high weeds had long ago killed off the lawn. Across the street sat a red-brick rambler with a well-trimmed yard and golden chain trees casting down their first blossoms. An ornate woodcut over the front door announced the family name as *Chang*. Looking at the clean lines of his neighbor's house, Paul felt as though the decay around him had suddenly worsened. He sighed and looked away, westward across the valley, to where the last arc of evening sun dipped behind the mountains. Above, the sky had turned to silver.

Lou walked out the front door, jumped down the steps, and sat down beside his father. "That's the last of the boxes," he said.

As though lost in thought, Paul merely nodded and continued to stare across the valley.

"When you think we'll be able to move in?" asked Lou.

Paul sighed. "I figure it'll take us two weeks to get it back in shape," he said, putting his arm around Lou's shoulder.

"Where we goin to camp till then?"

"State park up the highway a few miles."

Lou nodded. "Is it weird to be back after all this time?"

"Nah. I have a lot of good memories from here. In fact, I wish I could've taken you up the canyon and shown you the park where I used to run as a boy."

"Why can't we go?"

"Mine bought the land. Private property now."

Lou seemed at first to want to argue the matter, but then he looked at his father's face and saw a sadness there, and so they merely sat side-by-side on the broken porch, saying nothing, content to watch the swallows loop and soar, black against the silver sky.

CHAPTER 5

*T*he day after landing at Ramstein, Jason had reconstructive surgery on his leg. He awoke with a cast from his ankle to his hip and a pain like a nail had been driven through his kneecap. For the next three days he lived in the recovery ward on the second floor of the hospital building. The room had a row of windows that looked southwest, away from the base, and in the evening Jason raised his bed to a sitting position and looked out over the German countryside, green with spring rain, and let the sunlight warm his face.

His thoughts ranged from excitement, even giddiness, about being alive and heading home, to wonder about the voice he'd heard. He couldn't see any way to explain it without invoking God, and yet in part he wanted to believe it had all been some mistake, a cosmic cross-wiring, and that soon God would realize, time would be re-spun, and this time Rodney would survive. But the thought was absurd. God didn't make mistakes. It was during these long days, as he struggled for understanding, that Jason first began to feel guilt—a sort of quiet but growing suspicion that somehow he'd survived at Rodney's expense. By his last day at Ramstein he could no longer think about the ambush at the wall without fierce ambivalence: gratitude for his life, anger and bitterness for his best friend's death.

■ ■ ■

A flight attendant steered Jason in his wheelchair through the Salt Lake City Airport and left him near the baggage claim, where Jason planned to meet his mom. He wore a heavy brace on his left knee and held crutches across the armrest of his chair. His beard, though it would never be thick, had grown long at his chin and sideburns. As he waited, he watched the businesspeople and the tourists rushing past. It felt surreal, sitting there among the civilians, his leg still aching from the surgery. Only two weeks earlier he'd been on a patrol in Afghanistan. Only two weeks earlier Austen had turned his ankle, they'd sat down behind a wall, and Jason had heard the voice.

"Jason!"

The call startled him, though he knew the voice at once. His mom, Nancy. He turned his wheelchair around and saw her pushing through a crowd. She looked the same as ever—tall, thin, warm face, kind eyes. She was smiling and laughing and crying all at once.

"You're home," she said. Jason started to stand, but she gently pushed him back into the chair and hugged him, stood back and looked at him, then hugged him again. "You're home," she said.

■ ■ ■

They passed the three-hour drive to Esperanza without talking much—not because Nancy didn't try, but because Jason had trouble keeping up his end of the conversation. When she asked him about what had happened in Afghanistan, he said without meaning to be rude that he wasn't ready to talk about it. He seemed to prefer staring out the window in silence, and Nancy felt it best not to push too hard.

At the Esperanza exit they turned off the state highway and followed the steep road down to a small town huddled in a saddle-shaped valley. Jason looked out at the rooftops, the high trees, the redbrick mine offices, and the roads curling up through the narrow canyons to the pit mines. *Population 1,821*, the welcome sign announced. *Birthplace of Esperanza Copper.* He was home.

The sunlight fell through the branches and glinted on the windshield as they drove through the neighborhoods Jason had known all his life. The houses they passed were small, built from brick or stone in the 50s, when the mine opened. Most had small raised porches with chairs facing out to the patched asphalt streets. Aside from the models of the cars and the occasional satellite dish, very little in the town had changed in the last several decades.

They turned onto Hollow Stone Drive and followed it south to where it ended at a gate and a grove of Russian olives. Beside the gate stood two signs, one of sheet metal, the other of wood. The metal sign read:

Esperanza Copper Property
Trespassers will be Prosecuted

Beside that, the wood sign, older and sun-bleached:

Fire Creek—½Mile

Beyond the gate the road, now just two dirt tracks with cheat grass growing between, cut behind a grove of Russian olives and disappeared into a small canyon.

The Changs' house was the last on the street, about fifty yards from the gate, and steep sunburnt hills and ridges dotted with scrub oak rose from the backyard. After Nancy parked in the carport, she helped Jason with his wheelchair, and then while she got the duffel bag from the trunk, he wheeled out to the drive to look out at the neighborhood he'd known all his life. Immediately he noticed something strange. At the house across the street, which had been vacant for as long as Jason could remember, the weeds had been cut down from the cracks in the driveway, and in front of the carport they'd been pressed down into two tracks by the comings and going of a car.

"What's going on over there?" asked Jason.

"Where?"

Nancy shut the trunk and walked to his side.

"Across the street. Looks like someone's been over there."

"I have no idea. Last I heard, Gene Coldwell's son owned it, but he went out to Kanab years ago."

Jason shrugged. "It's probably just some kids checking the place out."

Nancy took one last look and then wheeled Jason to the front door, and when she opened it a crowd gathered in the living room and let out a chorus of welcome shouts. Behind them, a bright *Welcome Home!* banner had been taped to the wall.

For a few bewildered seconds Jason seemed not to know how to respond, but then at last he remembered to smile.

■ ■ ■

He's dead, Chang! Davison screamed, trying to pull Jason away from Rodney, back to the safety of the wall. There's nothing you can do!

No! Jason tried to tear free of Davison's grip. Let me go!

Jason! screamed Davison, but the voice was shifting, the images blurring. Jason . . . Jason?

Jason opened his eyes. He was lying on the couch, a sheen of sweat on his forehead, the TV on but muted across the room. His left leg ached from the strain of his tensed muscles. Nancy stood over him, her hand on his shoulder, worry sketched across her face. Above the couch on the wall hung the *Welcome Home!* sign from the party earlier that afternoon, and in the corner two helium balloons drooped toward the floor.

"Are you okay, Jason?"

"You just . . . you just startled me."

Slowly, Jason sat up, wiped the sweat from his forehead, and tried to stretch the ache out of his leg. Nancy sat beside him.

"Alison just called," she said.

Jason looked at her.

"She's on her way over."

"I thought she was away at school."

"She drove out to see you."

"I look like a mess. She won't even recognize me."

"I'm sure she's just happy you're okay."

Jason said nothing. They sat there, watching a soundless commercial on the TV.

"We haven't really talked about anything," Nancy said.

"I know. I'm sorry, Mom."

"Can I help?"

"I don't even know where to start."

"I love you, Jason. You know I'll do anything I can."

"I just need time to figure things out. There's more to what happened than what I told you on the phone."

Nancy smiled, a bit sadly, hugged Jason, and stood to leave.

"You know where to find me when you're ready."

The doorbell rang.

"I'll leave you two alone," Nancy said, and she disappeared up the stairs.

Jason stood, grimaced as his knee took his weight, and limped over to open the door.

Almost before it had fully opened, Alison jumped up the last step and hugged him. Then she pulled back, looked him over, and kissed him quickly, almost shyly, on the mouth.

"Can I still do that?" she asked, smiling a coy smile.

A bit startled, Jason merely looked at her for a time. She was pretty—Jason had almost forgotten how pretty—and he wanted to kiss her back. But for some reason he didn't: he just smiled and said, "You just did."

"I can hardly believe you're really home."

"It's only been eight months."

"Eight months is a long time."

Jason didn't know what to say to this, so he took a different tack.

"You can come in . . . if you want."

Alison stepped in and Jason shut the door. As he limped back to the couch, Alison watched his uneven step, grimacing as if it hurt her as much as it did him.

"How is it?" she asked.

Jason settled down at the end of the couch, and she sat beside him.

"Could be worse, I guess," he said, shrugging. "The shrapnel messed up my knee, but I've got a decent chance at full recovery."

"Does it hurt?"

"Not much."

As though to prove it, Jason stretched and flexed his knee a few times. Without warning, Alison raised a hand and touched Jason's beard, causing him to flinch a little.

"Not a bad look for you. Kind of lumberjack-ish."

"Thanks."

She lowered her hand and put it over his, but he didn't do much to reciprocate; he simply let her hand rest there.

"I just can't get over the fact that you're right here, sitting with me," Alison said.

"It's crazy."

"So what happens now?"

"No idea."

"You're not going back to Afghanistan, right?"

"This pretty much ends any military career," Jason said, pointing to his knee.

"You could come out to school with me in the fall."

Jason hesitated. "Hadn't thought about that."

"What else would you do? Stay here in Esperanza and work at the mine?"

"No. I don't know. I just . . ."

"So you come out with me. I know some guys you could room with, and the people on campus are really cool. I could even help you fill out the online application."

"I don't know," Jason said, trying his best not to make it sound like a rejection, even though he knew it was. He wanted in a way to be with Alison—they'd shared so much together before he left for the Marines—but he felt strangely disconnected, almost like he was watching this scene unfold and not living it. This was not the way he'd always imagined seeing her again.

"What's not to know?" Alison asked.

"I just barely got home, Alison."

It was too sharp, not how he meant it, and he saw the change immediately on her face, felt her take hand away from his. It was a stupid thing to say, he knew, but he couldn't see any way out of it. He felt suddenly very tired.

"Should I not have come?" asked Alison, and her tone was different now, guarded.

"It's not like that."

"Then what is it like?"

"I don't know."

"And us? Your last letter . . . That was only a month ago . . . I thought . . ."

Jason looked at her, wanting to say something, feeling too tired to think of the right words.

"I drove all the way back here just to see you," she said.

"I know. I know."

"Is what we were writing about still bothering you."

"It's different now . . ."

"I told you that wasn't an issue for me. You're a good person, Jason. That means way more to me than you doubting there's a God."

"You don't understand. Things have changed."

"So talk to me. Help me understand."

"I . . . I heard a voice."

Alison sat up straight and looked closely at him. "A voice?"

"You think I'm crazy."

"No, I don't."

"I shouldn't have said anything."

"I just want to be here with you."

Jason sighed, slouched back into the couch, and ran his hands down his face. "I'm sorry, Alison. I don't think I can do this. Not right now, anyway."

For a moment Alison was quiet. Then she stood.

"I understand." She looked at Jason; he didn't look back. "I'm heading back to school tomorrow morning. Give me a call at my dorm and we can talk."

"You don't have to leave."

But she was already walking to the door. "The semester's over in a few weeks and then I'm coming back to waitress for the summer."

"I'm serious, Alison. You really can stay."

Alison sighed, looked at him sadly, and again Jason felt a pressure in his chest seeing how pretty she was.

"I'm glad you're home safe, Jas. I said a lot of prayers for you."

He wanted to thank her, call her back, kiss her. Tell her that his best friend had taken the bullet meant for him and that it was tearing him up. But she was gone. Hearing her car back out of the driveway, he lay back on the couch and stared up at the homecoming banner. In the corner the balloons were almost touching the floor now. He closed his eyes, pulled a pillow over his head, thought of Rodney's wife and daughters, and let the guilt wash through him.

■ ■ ■

He meant to lie there for some time, but a few minutes later, there was a sharp knock on the front door, followed by four long rings of the bell. The door had an inset pane of colored glass, and when Jason opened his eyes to look, two wide eyes ringed by cupped hands and a pug nose were pressed against it.

"Rooster," Jason said, shaking his head.

The eyes watched Jason as he limped across the room, turned the lock, and opened the door. There on the doorstep stood a plump man about Jason's age, dressed in camouflage pants and a black t-shirt that said *Conspiracy*. He stepped inside without a word and, breathing hard, went straight to the couch and plopped himself down.

"How are you, Rooster?" said Jason, smiling a little in spite of himself. "Come on in and have a seat."

He shut the door and sat down across from Rooster, who was now looking over the living room point by point, as though memorizing its layout. His real name, which no one ever used, was Abednego (his father ran the local grocery store, called The Rooster's Market, from which the local kids had taken the nickname). Over the years Jason had seen him swallow whole goldfish, work for several months to build a life-size bust of Captain James T. Kirk with used chewing gum, run screaming down the street in his boxers during a blizzard (a test of endurance, he'd later said). A nice guy, though, despite it all—the kind who'll go miles out of his way for you. Shortly after Jason joined the Marines, Nancy had written that Rooster had followed his lead and joined the Navy. Must be on shore leave, Jason thought.

"So . . ." Rooster said, at last acknowledging Jason, "things go well with Alison?"

"What?" Jason said, caught off-guard.

"It just seemed like she didn't stay that long, that's all."

"Things went fine. And I'm not ever going to ask how you know how long she was here."

"Cool. But I'll tell you if you want."

"I don't think I want to know. Did you come by just to ask about that?"

"No," whispered Rooster, leaning forward in his chair like a conspirator. "We got new neighbors."

"What?"

"New neighbors, man. In the old house across the street. One boy, about twelve, and what I figure to be his dad, probably in his thirties. They been coming in every morning and working, and last night at twelve thirty of the a.m. they unloaded and didn't leave till about an hour ago."

"Wait, wait, wait. You were watching the street at twelve thirty a.m.?"

"Always do. I listen to Art Bell on XM and surveil the street for activity."

"What kind of activity?"

"You know, man. *Activity*."

"You haven't changed a bit," said Jason, shaking his head. "Except for a little padding around the middle. Doesn't the Navy have physical fitness?"

"Out of the Navy."

"You're out? How'd you get out?"

"I was getting too close to some big guns, man. They dumped me on some catch-22 stuff. Said I was 'mentally unfit for the rigors of combat.' Truth is, I was too fit. I knew things."

Here we go, Jason thought to himself, but aloud he simply asked, "So who do you think they are?"

"Hard to say." As Rooster spoke, he stood, walked to the window, shut the blinds, then parted them carefully, peeked out, and gave an all-clear sign. "I have a few guesses, though. You know anything about them?"

"Nope"

"Why not?"

"Why would I?"

"You live across the street."

"I didn't even know they were here."

Rooster peeked through the blinds once more and then sat down.

"I heard about what happened to you from your mom." Rooster sat down again on the couch. "How's the leg?"

"Little stronger every week."

"What about you?"

"Me?"

"Yeah. How you holding up?"

"I get by."

"Any plans?"

"Maybe."

"Which means 'no,' I assume. That being the case, you might be interested in the boxing tournament down at Fat Sammy's place. He needs some temps to help set up and run the show."

"I thought they shut that circus down."

"Sammy hired himself an attorney and got it back. Says it's going to be bigger than ever this year. They got a pretty big purse for the winner. I thought you might want to get out and work."

"I'll think it over."

Rooster stood and clapped Jason on the back. "Good to have you back, bro. Let me know if you get anything else on the neighbors."

"Will do."

"Mind if I go out the back?"

"Wouldn't have it any other way."

"Thanks, bro."

Rooster held out a fist for Jason to hit, and then they went through the kitchen to the back door. "I got to get out of here," muttered Jason, watching Rooster jog through the neighbor's backyard. The back of his t-shirt: *No Coincidences.*

CHAPTER 6

Most of his closest friends had all gone away to college or to out-of-town jobs, and those who'd stayed now worked full-time shifts at the mine. Although a few called him up to say hey, none of them stopped by. With his mom working as a paralegal in nearby Manti, he spent most of his hours alone.

On one of the first mornings he picked up the phone, called an operator, and got the number for Rodney and Erika Taylor in Las Vegas. He dialed but hung up before it could go through. For a minute or so he sat there staring at the phone. Then he dialed again. He didn't know what he wanted to say, but still he felt compelled to call. After five rings a machine picked up. A woman's voice started the message, with her two daughter's joining in halfway through to shout their names: "Hi, you've reached Erika . . . Nisha! . . . and Natalie! . . . Taylor. Leave us a message and we'll call you back."

Jason hung up and sat back on the couch, staring up at the ceiling.

His knee was healing quickly now, but with nowhere to go he passed the hours reading books from his father's library, which Nancy still kept neatly arranged in the office, just as it had been nearly twenty years earlier when Jason's father, Jeong, had been killed in an explosion at an Esperanza Copper warehouse. That was the same week that Jason, only eleven months old, had taken his first steps. Jason had no memory of his father, but in some way he couldn't quite define he'd always missed him. He thought about him every time he was asked about his Asian bloodline and forced to say he didn't really know anything about his Korean relatives—or Korea itself, for that matter.

Many of his father's books were written in Korean, and those in English dealt almost entirely with Jeong's main interest: warfare. He knew the reason only secondhand through his mother. The first twenty years of Jeong's life had been jarred several times by the forces of international conflicts. Jeong's parents had fled the war in Northern Korea in 1951 and had eventually found a home in Thailand, where Jeong was born. Jeong's father, Yo-han, had found employment at a U.S. Air Force base as a cook during the build-up to the Vietnam War, but then in 1968, he, along with several Americans, had been killed when a helicopter in a routine training flight had crashed into the kitchen where Jeong worked. As part of a compensation plan, the American Embassy arranged for Jeong and his mother to immigrate to the United States. Jeong's mother, however, never recovered from her husband's death, and she died of heart failure only two years later. Jeong ended up with a foster-care family in Utah, where he learned English, eventually met Nancy, and started work at the mine. And although he was happy in his new life, he never learned to forget how that war had turned his course far from what it might have been.

Sometimes in the late morning hours, after Jason awoke from his recurring dreams of Rodney's death, he would take down the Korean books from the case and look at the characters penned into the margins, at the signature and date on each title page. Jason had never learned to read Korean, but he took some comfort in his father's writing itself. Several times he lightly traced the characters with a pencil, marveled at the penmanship, wondered what his father had been thinking as he wrote, wondered what insights they might reveal into the man he'd always missed but never known.

At night he stayed up late with Letterman, Leno, or Conan. He ate little. Nancy joked that with his rough beard he looked like a hippie. She tried several times to talk to him, but each time he shut her out, told her that he wasn't ready. Of course, this only heightened her concern, led her to wonder if he was depressed, if perhaps she should take him to see a doctor, but in the end she decided to keep praying for him and hope that he could sort things out on his own.

One morning near the end of his first week home, as he was eating a late breakfast alone, the TV playing in the background, one of Jeong's war books on the table in front of him, he happened to look out the window and see a firmly-built man and a boy with thick glasses working in the yard, chopping down the tall weeds with machetes. So Rooster was right. What had brought them to such a broken house after it had been abandoned for so long Jason couldn't guess. It was the first time he'd ever seen anyone there. He shrugged and went back to his reading.

That same evening a pair of officers from Camp Williams—a lieutenant and a captain—visited and presented him a purple heart. Normally, they said, the award should have been given in ceremony before he got home, but someone had dropped the ball. They also confirmed that because of the damage to his knee, he would be honorably discharged.

"Of course, this don't mean we don't want you or nothin like that," said the captain. He was sitting across from Jason and Nancy in the living room. "It's just policy. Time for you to move on to other things."

"Understood," said Jason. "I already figured as much."

But the captain seemed to feel he had to reinforce the point, take Jason's self-esteem up a rung. "The good Lord brought you along this far," he continued. "I'm sure he'll take you on to do good things in civilian life."

Jason stood and looked at Nancy.

"I'm not feeling too great," he said. "I'm gonna go lie down."

He limped from the room without another word, leaving the officers to stare after him.

Later, Nancy came up to his room and found him on his bed, reading. The cover showed three men huddled in a trench, a mortar shell exploding in the background. Jason didn't look up from the pages.

"Is that one of Jeong's books?" she asked.

"Yeah. Found it a few days ago."

Nancy sat down at the desk and watched her son.

"I told the officers you were just getting over a nasty case of the flu," she said, forcing a smile. "I think they bought it."

"Thanks," said Jason.

He turned a page, scanned it, then turned a few more.

"They told me your disability pension should start next month. The amount'll depend on your final disability rating. They're also going to mail you some information on your college funding options."

"Why go back to school when I can live like a king in Esperanza on disability checks?"

Nancy sighed. She waited but Jason didn't look at her.

"You know I'm worried about you," she said at last.

"Yeah."

"You've lost a lot of weight."

Jason turned the page.

"I can't help you if won't tell me what's wrong."

Jason tossed the book to the floor. He put his hands behind his head, closed his eyes, and for a time said nothing at all. Then he described Narang, the heat, the wall where they sat down to eat. Almost whispering, he described the warning voice that seemed to come from within his own head. He described the momentary confusion as he tried to find its source. Then he told her about the single shot that took out Rodney, the bullet that killed the closest thing to a brother he'd ever had. He told her about Rodney's dead eyes. He told her about getting knocked out by an RPG blast.

"I wake up in the med unit. They ship me home. Here I am."

For a time Nancy was quiet. Jason lay on the bed, unmoving, waiting.

"My uncle had a similar experience," she said at last. "That was in France in World War Two."

"I remember the story," said Jason. "Him and his grunts are sleeping in a vacant barn. He wakes up and feels panicked but doesn't know why. He gets everyone up and says they're moving to a new position. A minute after they leave the Germans ambush the town and the barn is the first thing to go."

"I didn't know you'd heard that story," said Nancy.

"You told it to me when you were trying to get me to believe in God."

"Didn't work too well, then, I guess."

"Those kind of stories only work on people who already believe."

"Do you believe in God now, Jason?"

"Yeah."

"Do you believe the voice you heard was from God?"

"Yeah."

"I don't understand. It should be a wonderful thing. He saved you."

"Exactly. He saved *me*—and I'm grateful, I really am. But that's also my problem."

Nancy sat back in her chair. She looked for a time at her son, still lying back on his bed, hands behind his head, eyes closed, face expressionless.

"I still don't understand," she said.

"Rodney didn't hear any voices."

Nancy brows furrowed and a slight frown found her lips.

"He had a crazy dream the night before," Jason continued. "He knew something bad was going down. But he still never saw it coming. No one did. No one except God."

Nancy looked as though she wanted to respond but seemed unable to find the right words.

"Rodney was a father and a husband." Jason opened his eyes and looked at Nancy. "He was actually doing something with his life. He actually believed. But God let him die and saved *me*. The agnostic. The one who walked away."

"Sometimes we don't understand," Nancy said, her voice quiet, pained. "Sometimes we just have to—"

"It was the same with your uncle, just like it was the same with all the other good soldiers you hear about in church who say God saved them. Great for them, but what about the millions who didn't hear voices, didn't get any holy warnings to duck and cover. You think they didn't have mothers and wives and children praying just as hard for them? You think there weren't just as many broken lives and dreams when those guys came home in a box?"

"What are you saying, Jason? Are you saying God killed all those people?"

"No, he didn't kill them—but he could've saved them and didn't and I have to know why. I have to know why I'm here and my best friend isn't. I have to know why my life mattered more than his."

Jason lay on the bed, eyes closed again. Speechless, Nancy took his hand and held it in her own.

"Maybe it was his time to go," she said.

"You don't understand. Dad would've understood."

"You didn't even know him," said Nancy, sitting back in her chair.

"I know more about him than you think."

"Your father made his peace with what happened."

"Then why did he keep buying all these war books?" Jason asked, pointing to the book on the floor.

"What do you want me to do, Jason? Do you want me to blame God?"

"It's not a question of blame, Mom. It's a question of motive. Why did I hear a voice and Rodney didn't? Why did God let Dad walk into the warehouse? It would've been so easy for Him to intervene."

Nancy stood and calmly pushed the chair into the desk and turned for the door. "I'm leaving now, Jason. I can't talk about Jeong's death this way. I just can't."

Jason's voice caught her before she made it out: "If you knew a good man was about to die tragically and you had the power to prevent it, would you do it?"

Nancy paused, hand on the doorknob, halfway out of the room. "I don't know enough to make those kinds of decisions."

"It's so easy it's not even a question! Do you save the innocent or don't you?"

"I'm not God!" She was almost shouting now, something she almost never did. "Things must look different from his perspective!"

"Would you at least tell the ones you saved why you did it?"

Nancy sighed and looked down at the book on the floor, at the soldiers huddled in fear near the exploding mortar. "I can't answer these questions for you, Jason. I wish I could, but I can't."

Through his anger and frustration Jason saw his mom standing there, her face pained, and he knew suddenly he'd pushed things too far. What had started as a question had turned into an attack.

"I'm sorry, Mom," he said, closing his eyes again. "I didn't mean to use Dad against you . . . I'm just . . . trying to figure this out."

"Where do you go from here?" asked Nancy, her voice quiet again.

"I need to visit Rodney's wife, tell her what happened."

"Where does she live?"

"Vegas."

Nancy thought for a time.

"You can take my car. I'll get a ride to work tomorrow."

"Thanks, Mom. I mean that."

Nancy smiled, turned to leave, but stopped.

"You know, you're right about one thing. You're a lot more like your father than I ever realized." She smiled, maybe a bit sadly, at her son. "I'm sure he's proud of you."

For a few seconds longer, she looked at him lying there, then she slipped out of the room and closed the door.

■ ■ ■

When she was gone, Jason picked up his book and tried to read, but he couldn't focus on the words. It was only eight o'clock in the evening, but once again he felt deeply tired—emotionally and physically. He put down the book and limped over to shut the blinds. Across the street, the man and the boy were working again, hauling huge sacks of garbage out of the house and throwing them into the back of a rusted green pickup with a "For Sale" sign. Jason watched them for a time, wondering who they were and what they were doing, until the man looked across the street and their eyes met. Embarrassed, he closed the blinds, turned off the lights, and lay down to try to find sleep.

■ ■ ■

The air was hot, stifling hot, unbreathably hot. A dirty VW Bug drove by. Jason picked up his M-16 and eyed the driver, put it down again when the car had passed. Rodney glanced over his shoulder at the other soldiers, then slid up close.

Hey, Chang, you mind if I ask you something?

Sure. Fire away.

You believe in dreams?

Sure, have em all the time, Jason said. All the time.

The words seemed to echo through the town, growing louder each second, filling the old mud-brick buildings. And then, at once, everything went still, no movement anywhere. Heat waves rising off the desert. Don't stand up.

No, said Jason, covering his ears. No, no, no!

Let's get this over with, said Rodney. Standing, he slung his pack around onto his shoulders and adjusted the straps. He turned and looked over the wall.

Then he dropped.

Jason screamed. Anger like he'd never known surged through him. He wanted to hurt, to maim, to kill. But the world wouldn't let him. It blurred, disappeared, and Jason swam in a sea of thick darkness. There was nothing. There was no one. No pain. No suffering. No tragedy. Nothing. He was fading out of existence. He was at peace.

And then he was back in the heat. He stood beside a wall. Close by sat a group of soldiers. At the near end of the group, a black man with a friendly face; beside him, a soldier with light brown hair and a face hinting at Asian ancestry. They were talking, but Jason couldn't hear the words. He knew only that he had to warn one of them.

He walked to the black man and whispered in his ears, Don't stand up. The black man seemed startled. He looked around but couldn't see Jason standing over him.

Let's get this over with, said the other man. He put on a pair of yellow sport sunglasses and stood and slung his pack around onto his shoulders. He turned and looked over the wall.

The bullet hit him in the side of the head.

Jason saw him drop, saw his sunglasses shatter against the ground. The black man grabbed him and screamed for a medic. Jason turned and walked away into the town. Things were as they should be.

CHAPTER 7

When Jason awoke his mother had already left for work. He showered, packed a bag, and then went out to the kitchen and ate a quick breakfast. As he was cleaning his dishes, he saw the gift bag and the note. Made from paper with a bright floral print and tied with a wide purple ribbon, the bag looked like something from a craft magazine. On the note his mother's neat cursive:

> *Hi, Jason. Hope the world seems a little brighter this morning. I noticed last night that someone seems to have moved in across the street. Can you believe that!? Anyway, I wanted to welcome them but my ride came too soon. Will you please run this bag over for me before you leave? Thanks, Mom. Ps. Alison called, wants you to call her back.*

Jason peeked into the bag: mint brownies and homemade caramels. Figuring that he probably owed his mother the favor, he went back to his room to get his shoes.

■ ■ ■

That same old pickup was parked in front of the carport, and in the yard, rolled like tortillas, lay several decaying carpets whose original color Jason couldn't guess. He walked to the front door, pushed the bell. No sound. He knocked and waited.

A moment later the thick man with buzzed black hair whom Jason had seen from his window opened the door. His clothes and bare forearms were covered with dust. Thirty-five to forty, Jason figured. Not very handsome, but strong.

"Can I help you?" the man asked. He held the door close against his body so that Jason couldn't see into the house.

"Got something here for you."

Jason held up the bag.

"I think you got the wrong house."

"No, it's a house-warming gift."

The man looked hard at Jason, then at the bag, then back at Jason.

"I'm Jason," Jason offered at last. "I guess we're neighbors now."

"Paul Coldwell," said the man. "My son Lou's in the back cleanin."

"What brings you out to Esperanza?" Jason asked, trying to sound casual.

"A job at the mine," said Paul, perhaps a little defensively. "That's all there is to it."

"Well it's nice to meet you," said Jason. He handed the bag to Paul, who untied the bow and looked inside.

"Brownies and caramels," Jason explained. "From my mom."

"Everyone round here so nice?"

"She's a member of the local Relief Society. She has to do this kind of thing or they fire her."

Paul didn't seem to get the joke, and they looked at one in another in awkward silence. Jason wondered if perhaps the man didn't want company. Or maybe he was just shy. Either way it was time to go.

"So welcome to the neighborhood, Paul," said Jason, "and I'll see you around."

He started down the porch steps, taking care not to put too much weight on his left knee.

"What'd you do to your leg?" asked Paul.

"A rock fell on it," Jason said, turning back.

"A rock?" asked Paul, making a circle with his arms as though hefting up a large boulder. "Like a big boulder?"

"Exactly," said Jason. He limped across the street and up the walkway to the front door. When he looked back, he saw Paul still standing on the porch, watching him.

"You live there?" Paul shouted.

"Yeah."

"How long?"

"All my life."

Paul nodded as though making some mental note. Jason almost asked a follow-up question, but decided it wasn't worth the effort. He waved to Paul and went inside.

A few minutes later he was on the highway, his bag in the passenger seat, the window open, wondering if he'd be welcome when he showed up at Rodney's house—no, at his wife's house. But, he supposed, it didn't make any difference. This was something he had to do.

CHAPTER 8

A floorboard groaned as Paul Coldwell walked the blue-black darkness of the hallway, the denim of his jeans swishing, a sheet of paper in his hand. Outside Lou's bedroom he stopped and looked in through the open door. The digital alarm clock next to the mattress lit the boy's face and the top folds of his blanket in a pale green glow. 4:47 a.m. Paul watched his son sleeping; he listened to the measure of his slow breathing and studied his palely lit face. At the window a soft breeze billowed the curtains. Paul held the notebook paper against the doorframe and quietly pulled the door shut on it.

On the front porch, he stood in the cool morning air and looked out at the flat black angles of the mountains drawn against a dim aurora. Across the street the Changs' windows were dark and the air was full of the rhythms of crickets. Gravel crunching beneath his boots, he walked to the carport, climbed into his pick-up, drove away into the darkness.

■ ■ ■

The clock had moved forward an hour-and-a-half when Lou awoke. He fumbled for his glasses, then rose and opened the bedroom door, loosing the notebook paper to glide down to the floor boards. He yawned and picked it up. The writing—large bold letters in a slow script—observed carefully the lines and margins of the torn page.

I am at my first day of work, as we talked about last night. You will find cereal in the kitchen for breakfast. I will return this afternoon. We will then work on the house and play a short game of catch or go for a walk. Hope you have a good day today. Love, Dad

Lou folded the note, left it on his blankets, and walked to the kitchen. When he flipped the switch, two florescent tubes pinged, flickered, and lit, scouring the kitchen with white light. Years ago the room would have been stylish and friendly, but now the old appliances, peeling laminate counters, and brown plastic tabletop were just worn and sad. Four chairs with cushions of cracked vinyl had been stacked one upside-down over the other against the wall. A stained square on the floor marked the place where the refrigerator would go if they had one, but for now they had only the mini-fridge on the counter near the sink. Stepping over the peeling seam of the olive-green linoleum, Lou walked to the cupboards and took down a bowl.

He made a breakfast of Shredded Wheat, the only cereal Paul had bought at Rooster's Market the day before, and a few mint brownies from the gift bag. He dressed and went to the living room, where he rummaged through boxes yet unpacked. In the second he found what he was looking for, an old photo album with a leather cover and tarnished brass corners.

He turned to a page near the beginning of the book, where a faded picture showed a young boy much like himself, though a little thicker through the limbs and darker in complexion. He stood in front of a fort, the kind boys often build from bits of scrapwood and two-by-fours. But this fort far surpassed the usual boyhood work. Ten feet wide, it seemed to have two rooms and a solidly built frame— well-matched corners, square windows, and an inclined roof with black shingles. The door, fastened with metal hinges, was open in the picture, offering a glimpse of a small table inside. In front of the fort, a fire-pit ringed by large gray stones. A grove of old pines cast irregular shadows over the roof and a ridge of broken rock loomed behind. The boy wore a long hunting knife on his belt. The caption:

Paul, 1981, Fire Creek.
He built this fort (with dad's help) from wood left over
from the house. It was quite a feat and took him all summer. Now
Paul and his friends spend nearly all of their waking hours there.
Dad and I think he has a future as an architect.

Lou slipped the picture from the plastic, carefully pocketed it, and returned the album to the box. The sun was still low in the sky when he shut the door behind him, jogged down Hollow Stone Drive, ducked under the locked gate, and rounded the bend toward the canyon.

■ ■ ■

The phone rang. Sleep-blind and clumsy, Jason searched the nightstand with his hand and at last found the receiver.

"Hello?" he rasped.

"This is your 8:00 wake-up call," a friendly computerized recording said. "For a ten-minute snooze, please dial 'one' now, otherwise—"

Jason hung up the phone and forced himself out of bed. The sun was already bright behind the old motel curtains, and when he drew them back the light made him squint. He'd arrived in Vegas the previous evening, eaten at a fast food chain, checked into a discount motel, then walked to a local barber shop for a haircut and a shave. Now, as he looked into the motel mirror, his clean face looked strange, too young and soft. But it was better this way. He didn't want to look like a bum when he met Rodney's wife.

In the motel office he found a local phone directory and tore out the page with the entry *Taylor, Rodney and Erika*.

Thirty minutes later he arrived at the address—a new condominium complex on the west side of the city. Jason checked his watch: 8:56. He parked outside the condo—number 112—turned off the engine and waited. Although it was already hot outside, several pairs of joggers were out on the path that circled the complex. People came out of their condos and got in their cars and drove away. Several eyed him suspiciously, but he was concentrating too hard on reviewing his mental notes for the conversation to notice.

At 9:05, he got out of his car, walked to the door, and knocked. A young girl, maybe four or five years old, answered it. She had long black hair, braided, four or five bright beads at the end of each strand. Jason knew as soon as he saw her that she was Rodney's girl, and seeing her brought a strange pressure into his chest, almost like he was being squeezed. "Is your mom home?" he asked quickly.

Leaving the door open, the girl ran back into the condo, shouting for her mom. A minute or so later Rodney's wife came to the door. She was a tall woman, athletic, light brown skin, brilliant hazel eyes. A confident woman in manner and movement. She looked at Jason as if puzzled by his presence. "May I help you?"

"I'm Jason Chang, a friend of Rodney."

The woman's smile disappeared.

Rodney had told her about him: Jason could see the recognition in her face. "Come in," she said.

Jason sat at the breakfast table across from Rodney's two daughters. The older of the two had answered the door, and she now sat sideways in her chair and stared at Jason without embarrassment. The younger one, perhaps three, sat on a phone book to reach the table and slurped cold cereal at a steady pace. The condo was small, but clean, with comfortably worn furniture. Black-and-white nature prints hung on the walls in plastic frames. Rodney's wife, Erika, poured a glass of orange juice, took a bagel out of the fridge, and set the food in front of Jason.

"I wish we had something better, but it's grocery day."

"This is perfect." Jason sipped the juice to prove it. All three of them watched him. He smiled awkwardly. "You're probably wondering what I'm doing here."

"The timing is surprising," said Erika, "but the visit isn't. Rodney said you two were like brothers."

Jason sighed and let his eyes wander the room. The mental notes he'd made only minutes before were gone. Erika watched him and waited, content to let him begin when he was ready. Eventually he decided it would be best to work up to it gradually, so he told her of his first days in Afghanistan, when he and Rodney had been assigned to the same patrol. He told her that over the next three months Rodney had become the closest friend he'd ever had. He told her that it was Rodney who'd invited him to the Christian meetings every Sunday and started him rethinking his own faith. He told her that Rodney spoke of them almost constantly, that he loved them very much.

He paused. The youngest girl had stopped eating and now sat on her phonebook watching him with wide dark eyes. The older girl had taken a seat on Erika's lap.

"Girls," said Erika, as though emerging suddenly from a dream, "go get your shoes on. I got to drop you off at daycare in five minutes."

Without complaint the girls got down from the table and walked to the back room. When they were gone Erika turned back to Jason. "I appreciate the gesture," she said quietly, "but we know Rodney loved us. You didn't have to come all this way."

"That's not the full reason I came," said Jason.

Erika sat back in her chair and with her hazel eyes considered her husband's old friend. "What *did* you come to say, Jason?" she asked, perhaps a bit reluctantly.

"I need to tell you how Rodney died."

"I know how he died," said Erika, but for the first time that morning her confidence seemed to wane. Something in the way her back straightened, in the way her lips pulled tight.

"If you don't want to hear this, I'll leave."

She gestured for him to continue, a movement hardly more than a raised finger. Jason drew in a slow breath. He started with the heat. Then their foolish stop at the wall. Then Rodney's dream.

"He knew," Jason said.

Erika kept her eyes on the table. Jason watched her and bitterness filled him. He told her about the voice.

Erika raised her head and their eyes met. "Jesus saved you," she said, her voice a whisper.

You've got it all wrong, Jason wanted to say. Jesus—whoever it was—had *not* saved Rodney. That was the important thing. That was what mattered.

"Rodney didn't hear the voice," he said.

Erika understood at last, and when she smiled it was in sadness. Gently she touched Jason's hand. "I can't claim to understand Jesus' ways. I can only tell you that he visited this house and healed my heart when I thought it would be broken forever. I *will* see my Rodney again."

Jason looked away. Of all people, she should understand the injustice of this, he thought. But even as the thought came he saw the contradiction, that he was asking Erika to share his misery and anger. He pushed his chair back and stood. "I shouldn't have come."

Erika offered no argument. She walked with him to the door, opened it, and let him out.

"I'm sorry we couldn't meet under different circumstances," Jason said. "Please tell your daughters goodbye for me." He started limping slowly back to the car.

"Jason."

He paused, looked back. Erika stood at the door watching him.

"Jesus saved you for a reason, you know." She smiled at him, a beautiful confident smile. "Rodney would've told you the same thing."

Jason turned away. He walked to the car and got in, and when he looked back the door to 112 was closed.

■ ■ ■

Paul Coldwell sat behind a small wooden desk next to a window streaked with hard-water stains. He hated first days, but this one was figuring to be especially bad. Another headache had kept him up late, and even after it had gone, worry over the new job kept sleep from him. He rubbed his eyes, looked around the room at the men who'd also come for first-day training. There were about fifteen in all, with nearly every race and age represented. At the front of the room three dark-haired Latinos sat together, their conversation jumping between Spanish and English. Near the door a tall black man leaned back on his chair, his feet propped up on the metal garbage can. In the seat immediately beside him, a bald man with a wiry red beard and eyes like slits in his face met Paul's gaze unflinchingly.

"Where you from?" he asked roughly.

"Me?"

"Yeah, you. I been tryin to figure you out. You ain't no Mexican and you sure ain't no Asian or black, but you don't look white neither what with the black hair and eyes."

Paul's expression did not change. "I'm from Kanab."

"So what then? You got some Navajo in you or something? Your daddy marry an Indian princess?"

Paul said nothing. He turned toward the window, pretended to look out at the parking lot.

"I asked you a question."

Before Paul could respond, the tall man near the door looked over: "What's your problem, Detner? The man obviously don't want to talk to you."

Detner raised his palms. "I was just curious. Why you people all got to be so sensitive about your race? I mean, geez. I'm full blood Viking and you don't see me all embarrassed about it."

He shook his head in disgust. Paul continued to stare out the window.

The door opened and a thin woman with dye-red hair entered. Wearing a green polo shirt emblazoned with Esperanza Copper's corporate logo, she walked to the television mounted on the wall at the front of the room and pushed a tape into the VCR. "You all have to watch this," she said without looking at them. "Boyd Grummet's your boss and he'll be here at the end of the video. You got a question, save it for Boyd."

She clicked on the television, switched off the light, and left the room. Paul slid his chair noisily back over the tile and slouched back to watch. In yellow titles the words *Welcome to Esperanza Copper* appeared against a grainy blue background. They faded and a plush office appeared—a darkly stained desk and plush leather chair, upon which sat a man whose push-broom moustache, brown plaid coat, and fat yellow tie dated the video at least twenty years.

"Hello," he said with slight accent. His body was rigid, his brown unblinking eyes staring out of the television. "My name is Flores . . ." A pause. He looked away from the camera, nodded, looked back. "*Luis* Flores and I am president and founder of Esperanza Copper, the company that you are of now a part . . . I mean, you are a part . . . eh, a part for." He paused, swallowed, wiped his forehead. "Let me take a while, eh, I mean a moment to tell you about our proud tradition."

Paul slouched back further.

"The word *Esperanza* in my language means *hope* and there is a very good reason why our town and company takes this name. When I came to this country from Spain in the early fifties, I was a poor geology student, and I had nothing. In fact, I had less than nothing . . ."

Paul closed his eyes and let his head fall back against the crown of the chair. From the front of the room the voice of Luis Flores droned on.

■ ■ ■

Morning sunlight slid down the face of the steep ridges towering above as Lou hiked a slow rise and came to a clearing. A quick-running creek shimmered down, curving in a series of S turns around a few splintered picnic tables. Warm patches of sunlight fell through the aspen, dappling the broken tabletops and the smudges of old firepits now overgrown with weeds. At the other side of the clearing, the dirt road continued up the canyon and disappeared into the trees.

Lou took out the photo. Because it had been taken from a distance of only fifteen feet or so, he couldn't place it within the wide view before him. He pocketed it again and walked up through the tables deeper into the canyon, to where the aspen quit and the pines took root. After a few minutes of searching he came to a trail marked by small rocks and followed it for about a hundred yards, passing a tree scarred with the block letters *GENE LOVES BRENDA*. A few more steps, and there on his right, the ridge from the photo's background came suddenly into view. And in front of it stood his father's boyhood fort, broken now, like some small, dilapidated house from a forgotten time.

The roof had long ago collapsed onto the warped and broken table and chairs. One of the walls had fallen outward, and the other three slouched against the closest pine. The wall had that had once divided the two rooms seemed to have disappeared.

Slowly, almost reverently, Lou walked to the ruins and stepped over the half-buried blackened rocks that marked his father's firepit. He hefted up the fallen door and looked beneath it. Black ants had built a nest in its shelter. When he let it drop again, dust rose into the streaks of sunlight. He circled the old fort, studying it from every angle. Milkweeds grew around the perimeter, and in the window of one of the fallen walls, a great brown and white spider perched at the center of its web, its legs stretched into an X.

Lou thought that perhaps he should feel disappointed by the decay: so many of his father's stories centered on this place, on that time. But he felt, instead, a flicker of hope. He would restore it exactly to his father's specifications. Then he would bring his father here, show him his childhood stories rebuilt, let him remember those happier times. He knew his father was deeply troubled—he'd heard him awake in the night, pacing, sometimes crying, thinking his son was asleep and unaware. Lou himself didn't fully understand how Fire Creek might help him face those troubles; he knew only that something was wrong and that this place had once mattered to his father. Perhaps it could again.

■ ■ ■

Luis Flores stared blankly out of the television: "Welcome, y bienvenido, to Esperanza Copper," he said, and the video abruptly ended. Slumped back in his chair, his mouth open, Paul slept. Beside him, Detner turned and whispered something to another new worker; then he slowly opened the lid of his desk, held it up for a moment, then slammed it down hard.

Paul's legs and arms shot out and his head jerked up and his chair tipped backward and he tried to re-balance himself by kicking his feet up but only succeeded in kicking the desk forward. Paul, the chair, and the desk fell clattering to the floor.

He lay there stunned, one leg propped over the fallen chair, the desk overturned at his feet. Most of the men in the room were laughing. Paul touched the back of his head, looked at his palm to see if there was any blood. It was clean. His lower lip twitched as he looked up at the men around him. His first thought was to let it go, to rearrange the desk and sit down and pretend nothing had happened. But the laughter, the eyes turned toward him, the pressure of the first day, the stress of the last months—it was all too much. His mind buzzed with rage. He kicked the overturned chair and sent it crashing into another desk. With both hands he pushed off the floor and jumped to his feet.

Surprised, the men cut their laughter short. Paul turned to Detner, his intent unmistakeable. One of the other new workers, an old Polynesian man with a kind brown face, raised both his hands to Paul. "Now just calm down, son. You don't want to do anything stupid."

But the anger was too strong to hold back, and Paul hardly noticed the old man. "*You* did that," he growled, pointing at Detner.

Detner backed away, bumped up against the desk behind him. "I didn't know you'd fall. We was just jokin around with you."

Paul didn't mean to do it. It just happened. He shoved Detner hard, knocking him backward over the top of a desk, which tipped over with a crash. Another worker managed to grab him around the shoulders and break his fall. Paul shoved the desk out of the way and would have swung again had not two workers held him back.

"Get off me," he shouted, trying to push past them.

By this time, Detner had regained his feet and stood wide-eyed, staring at Paul. "He hit me!" he shouted lamely, his face flushed. "He just hit me!"

The door slammed open. A thin man in company uniform stood in the doorway, a stack of files in his arms. The nametag on his chest: Boyd Grummet. Seeing him, Paul backed away from Detner and the two men who had held him and stumbled against the overturned chair. Brow furrowed and lips pressed into tight frown, Grummet took in the scene with a slow sweep of his eyes, lingering for a moment on Paul, then on Detner. He walked to the table at the front of the room and slapped the files down.

"Get this room fixed up," he said. "Then find your files and fill out your personal information and your tax forms." He pointed to Paul and Detner. "You two come with me."

Grummet walked out of the room. Without a word Paul and Detner followed.

They walked to Grummet's office, where Paul and Detner sat across from the desk. Grummet opened a file drawer and took out two yellow papers. Paul watched him. His face was long, creased around his eyes and mouth, completely unreadable.

"Names?" he said, sitting.

"Detner Tinsdale."

"Paul Coldwell."

Grummet looked hard at each man in turn. He was a hard man with a face out of an old cowboy movie.

"You boys know I should fire both your butts right now," he said at last.

Paul looked down at the floor.

"I been here thirty years," he continued, "and you can bet your mama's house I don't have to put up with this kind of asinine stunt."

Paul spoke very quietly: "I need this job."

"Why should I care?"

"I got a son. If I don't work he won't be able . . ." Paul paused and looked down at the floor. "I need this job."

"If I don't give it to you?"

"I'll clean bathrooms, anything. This was all just a mistake."

Boyd nodded, flicked his pen around his thumb, turned his attention to Detner. "What about you? You got anything to say."

"He's crazy," said Detner. "He tried to kill me back there."

"What're you talkin about?" Paul cut in. "You're the one who threw me out of my chair."

"I didn't—"

"Just shut up!" shouted Grummet. He considered the two men for what seemed a long time. Then he pushed the yellow papers across the desk. "Fill these out."

Detner took a pen from the cup on the desk. Paul glanced at the paper, then at Boyd.

"What's this?"

"Disciplinary warning. Goes in your file. You see another one of these anytime soon and you're out the door no questions asked."

His mouth pressed into a tight frown, Paul studied the form a moment longer. Then he took a pen from the cup and set to work.

When both men had finished, Boyd led them back to the training room. Paul walked a few paces behind, and as he passed an announcement board, the header of a bright yellow flyer caught his eye. He slowed his pace.

Fat Sammy's Annual Boxing Tournament is Back!!!!
$2000 First Prize
Tournament begins Friday, July 24
Behind Fat Sammy's Bar and Restaurant
Register at Fat Sammy's

The address and phone number were listed at the bottom. Paul looked down the hallway: Detner and Boyd had turned the corner. Quickly, he tore off the flyer, crumpled it into his pocket, and hurried to catch up.

CHAPTER 9

*I*n the late afternoon Lou left Fire Creek. He walked the right track of the rutted country road beneath the aspen, heading back to the gate and the neighborhood. The afternoon sun was bright, the air fresh and hot. Insects buzzed in his ears. Two scrub Jays flew screeching overhead—twin blurs of deep blue. He felt good walking the old trail. He thought of his father, years ago, kicking up the same dust, hopping over the same gullies, looking up at the same ridgelines. He thought eagerly about the day, a few weeks from now, when he would bring his father here.

When he'd come down within two-hundred yards of the gate—he could see the rooftops now between the branches ahead, a truck engine sounded somewhere in the distance behind him. He spun back and looked up the road. A truck came over a rise about three-quarters of a mile back, just past Fire Creek. The driver saw him, leaned on the horn for a few seconds, and made some sort of crazy hand signal out the window. Lou stood where he was. The truck accelerated. He knew he was in trouble.

He ran.

■ ■ ■

Jason had driven without rest from Vegas, but the trip still seemed endless. In the wide sagebrush deserts between towns, when he couldn't get a radio station, his thoughts had invariably turned back to Erika's last comments. In his mind he pictured a great cosmic ledger, with a debt penned in red ink beside his name. It was a lonely drive, full of self-doubt, regret, and fear, but also of grim acceptance. Even though Erika had made her peace with things, the facts were still the same: God had saved him, and he wanted to know why. What did God want from him? He parked in the garage and got out of the car.

"What's up, bro?"

The sudden voice made Jason jump. He spun around to see Rooster standing there, holding a package, grinning like a crescent moon.

"What are you doing, Rooster?" Jason asked, trying to mask his fright.

Rooster tossed the packaged to Jason. "It's from Alison. Mail dude brought it this morning but you guys weren't home."

"Why did you have it?"

"You didn't want it sitting on your porch all day, did you? That's just an open invitation for thieves."

"Um, thanks, I guess."

"No es nada, amigo. Oh, and I almost forgot—I talked to Sammy for you. He's got you down for working the tournament. He'll call you this week."

Then, with a quick salute and an about-face, Rooster was gone, running down the driveway and back to his own house down the street.

Jason looked after his friend and shook his head, then he went inside, got the cordless phone from the kitchen, and took it and the package out to the porch bench. Inside the package he found a card and leather-bound copy of a book called *Jesus the Christ.* He thumbed through the book, then turned to the card.

Dear, Jason. Been thinking about you since we talked. Don't want to be preachy, but this book has helped me a lot. Maybe it can help you too. Looking forward to talking after you get things figured out. —Alison

"After I get things figured out," Jason said aloud. He looked at the book again, then put it and the card back in the box. For a time he sat there, unmoving, thinking; then he picked up the phone and dialed. As it began to ring, a strange thing happened: beyond the end of the paved street, the new boy from the Coldwell place raced in high gear around the trees and ducked under the gate. As Jason watched, he sprinted the last fifty yards to his house. Redfaced, breathing hard, his glasses slipping down his nose, he paused on the porch and locked eyes with Jason and seemed about to say something, but then a truck revved from the dirt road near the gate and he stepped inside and slammed the door.

The phone quit ringing and Alison picked up: "Hello?"

But now a white pickup with Esperanza Copper logos on the panels came fast around the trees, throwing up a wall of dust.

"Hello?"

Jason looked at the phone, then back at the truck, which stopped at the gate while the passenger jumped out, unlocked, and opened it. They were obviously after the kid.

"Anybody there?" Alison said, then the phone went dead. Jason glanced at it again, then hit the end button. He'd have to call her back. Meanwhile, the truck was driving slowly down Hollow Stone Drive, the two men inside scanning from side to side. When they neared Jason's house they pulled to the curb.

"You see a kid come through here?" the driver asked through the open window.

"Why?" asked Jason. "He in trouble?"

"We seen him up on mine property."

"So? You all aren't doing anything up there."

"Whether we are or not don't matter. The signs are posted and they ought to mean something."

The passenger leaned across and said, "Skinny kid, maybe thirteen or fourteen, big old glasses." He held his looped fingers to his eyes.

Jason hesitated. He felt reluctant to tell them, a sort of vague discomfort in the back of his mind. Maybe it was the truck driver's attitude.

"He came through just before you boys," he said at last.

"You see where he went?"

"Ran to the Montgomerys' house and jumped their fence." Jason pointed down the street to a two-story with a wood-panel fence.

"Thanks, buddy."

The driver shifted into gear and accelerated, leaving Jason at the curb. He watched them until they turned the corner at the Montgomerys'. When he looked across at the Coldwell place he caught a glimpse of the boy's face in the window before it pulled back. Since Jason still had the cordless and didn't want to spend energy taking it back inside, he did the next best thing. He opened up the mailbox and slipped it in over the day's mail, figuring no one would find it there. Then he walked across the street and knocked on the Coldwells' door.

After a short time he cupped his eyes and leaned close to the dirty glass panel. The house inside was dim, and he could just make out bare floorboards, moving boxes piled in the corner, and a picture frame, about six-inches square, mounted on the near wall. No sign of the boy. Jason knocked harder. "If you want, I can just wait until your dad gets home!"

A few seconds later the lock jiggled and the door opened. The boy's hair was stuck to his forehead with sweat, and his green eyes were small behind the plastic lenses. He was skinny and disheveled, dressed in an overlarge T-shirt, white denim pants that hadn't reached his ankles in at least a year, and dirty high-tops. He pushed his glasses up his nose with his index finger and smiled. Jason liked the kid almost instantly: something about his complete lack of style and awkward demeanor.

"Hey, Jason," the boy said.

"How you know my name?"

"It was on the card you brought over with them treats. My name's Lou."

"Some guys just drove by looking for you, Lou."

"I seen em. You sent em down the street."

"Any idea why?"

"Cause you're nice?"

"No, not why I sent them on—why they were looking for you."

Lou shrugged.

"Look. If I wanted to get you in trouble, I wouldn't have fed those guys a line."

"All right, I was looking for a place my dad used to go to when he was a kid."

"Your dad lived in Esperanza?"

"This was his house—or his mom and dad's, anyway."

"And where was this place he went?"

"Up by Fire Creek."

"The old park?"

"You know about it?"

"I grew up here."

"You know why they closed it off?"

Jason explained that a secondary mine had been planned for the southeast mountains, but the copper markets had turned sour and the park sat up there unused. The mine, however, having already built a new park, refused to take down the fences and gates, saying that eventually the new copper pit would be opened. When Jason explained that they'd just started doing land surveys on the back of the mountain and used the road daily now, disappointment showed on Lou's face.

"You plan on going up there again?" Jason asked.

Lou hesitated. Jason felt that the boy was trying to decide how far to trust him. After a few seconds, he made his decision: he told Jason about Paul's old fort and his plans for it. As Jason listened, he sensed from the slow quiet manner in which Lou spoke of his father and Fire Creek that somehow it went deeper than a few childhood memories.

"How you plan to get all your tools and supplies up there without getting caught?"

Lou looked up, eyes wide behind his glasses, several emotions crisscrossing his face, the most obvious of which was desperation. "I don't know," he said finally, slouching in defeat.

Jason studied the boy, his old clothes, his clunky glasses, his worn shoes. The hard defiance chiseled into many kids his age was completely missing. Jason felt sorry for him, alone as he was in the rundown house, his plans for his father suddenly crushed. He decided to tell him.

"There's another path to Fire Creek."

Lou looked up.

"Behind the Martins' house," Jason added.

"Where's that?"

"On Prospector Way."

Jason squatted and drew a map with his finger on the dirt gathered at the corner of the porch. He marked a line for Prospector Street and at the end of it another perpendicular line representing a chain-link fence. He then drew a rectangle, and between the rectangle and the fence line, a circle. The rectangle represented the Martins' house, Jason explained, and the circle a willow tree, behind which Lou would find a spot where he could slip under the fence. "If it's still there, anyway," Jason added, looking down at his map. "I haven't been there in a while. On the other side of the fence is a trail that'll take you up to the picnic grounds the back way, where you can't be seen from the road."

"How you know about it?"

"Me and my friends made it when I was your age."

Lou looked at Jason with newfound respect. "What's the street called again?" he asked. "Poor Settler?"

"Pro-spec-tor."

"Got it," said Lou. "And help me out with the tree."

"Willow."

"What do they look like?"

"Big and wide with long leafy things hanging down. Sort of shaped like a giant mushroom."

"Got it," said Lou. "I go down to Cross-secting Street and look for a giant mushroom tree. Easy."

"Close enough," said Jason.

Lou pushed his glasses up again and studied the lines in the dirt. "Or maybe you could take me down there sometime and just show it to me?"

"Sure," said Jason, surprised. He hadn't expected the kid to invite him along, and as much as he liked him, he didn't really want to go on any day trips. "Maybe we could do that sometime."

"How bout tomorrow?" said Lou.

"Tomorrow," Jason repeated. "Tomorrow I might have some work to do."

"What if we went early?"

"Listen, Lou, just stop by sometime and knock and I'm sure we can figure something out. My schedule's a little crowded and unpredictable."

The boy held out a hand to Jason as though they were now friends. Jason smiled and slapped him five.

"I'll see you later, then, Jason."

"See you."

When he got home again, Jason made himself quesadillas in the microwave and took out Alison's book and sat down at the kitchen table. He'd not yet completed the third sentence, however, when he was interrupted: the garage door opened and Nancy entered, her briefcase in one hand, a few letters and the cordless telephone in the other.

"Strange delivery today," she said, seeing Jason at the table. "Any idea who it might be from?"

Jason looked up from his book. The phone. He'd forgotten. "I left it out there," he said.

"In the *mailbox*?"

"I didn't want someone to steal it," said Jason, reading again.

"So you put it in the mailbox?"

"Yeah," said Jason, as if the point were obvious.

Nancy laughed, shook her head, and set the phone down on the base. She sat across from Jason at the table. "So don't just sit there reading. Tell me how things went in Las Vegas?"

Jason looked up from his book and realized that he had no idea how to answer the question.

■ ■ ■

That evening when Paul came home, Lou could see he was tired, perhaps a bit discouraged too, although he offered no complaints. Instead he took the bread, cheese, and ham out of the minifridge and threw together a dinner of sandwiches and saltine crackers. They took chairs out to the back porch, where they could eat in the fresh air and sunlight.

Lou raised his sandwich to take his first bite, but Paul stopped him.

"Prayer, first," he said.

The sandwich went back to the plate.

"Your turn," said Paul.

Lou offered a short prayer, in which he thanked God for beautiful weather and good food and Paul's job, and then, more earnestly, almost whispering, he prayed that his father's headaches and upset stomachs might quit.

"Thank you," said Paul, when he'd finished.

They ate. After a time, Lou brushed the crumbs from his lips and turned to his father. "How come you started us prayin all of a sudden?"

"We've prayed for a long time," said Paul.

"First prayer I ever heard you say was in Melvin's motel only a few months ago."

Paul sighed. "I guess I felt like it couldn't hurt." For a moment, he seemed lost in thought, but then he turned to Lou and smiled, took a bright flyer out of his pocket and passed it to Lou. "What do you think of that?"

"A boxing tournament?" Lou asked, looking it over.

"Two thousand bucks for the winner."

Lou looked up from the flyer.

"Been a while since you boxed."

"It don't matter. I can still beat anybody around here easy."

"What about your headaches?"

"I know how to keep my bell from gettin rung. Be as safe as a walk in the park."

Lou reread the flyer, then looked back at his father. Paul could see what he was thinking.

"Okay," he said, raising his hands. "I'll see if they'll let me wear a sparring helmet."

Lou's expression didn't change.

"Listen," said Paul, his voice serious and lecturing now, "if I can win this thing and get the truck sold, that's almost a quarter of what we need." Paul stopped suddenly, as though checking his own thoughts. "It could really help us out, that's all."

Before Lou could say anything more, Paul grabbed the flyer and stuffed it back into his pocket, then he took their empty plates and asked, "So you still up for that game of catch?"

Lou said that he was and went back to his room to find their gloves and ball. Paul watched him, and then as a second thought shouted, "After that we better work on the yard some more. I don't want the neighbors thinkin we plan to live with this mess."

For a half-hour or so they stood out in the street and threw the ball. Later as the cool evening breeze blew down from Fire Creek canyon, Paul found a few rusted gardening tools in the carport and they set to work pruning the deadwood from the maple.

CHAPTER 10

*L*ou awoke in the morning dark when he heard Paul start the truck. Briefly, the headlight shone across the window, lighting the old curtains and casting strange shadows on the walls. The engine backfired, accelerated, and faded. Then the quiet of crickets. He tossed aside his quilt, sat up, yawned, and felt for his glasses.

A moment later, dragging one of the old vinyl chairs with him, Lou took his Shredded Wheat bowl into the living room and sat near the open window, next to the old stone fireplace. Across the street the Changs' house was dark, quiet, the shadowed branches of the Japanese maple shivering with a soft wind, the warm light of the nearby streetlamp just touching the corner of the picket fence. He'd finished about half the bowl when one of the Changs' lights came on behind the slats of the Venetian blinds. He left his cereal on the windowsill and ran to his room to get dressed.

On Hollow Stone Drive, in the dim predawn light, a few sprinklers now ratcheted lazily over the Chang's lawn. Lou stood at the curb in front of the house and timed his run through the sprinklers, up the walkway and to the doorstep. When the moment came, he sprinted up the cobblestones and tried to clear the three porch steps with a single leap, but he came up just short: his foot caught the top stair and he more or less rolled onto the porch, nearly overturning a pot full of geraniums. He jumped up, straightened his shirt, and quickly scanned the Changs' windows. No one had seen or heard him. And he'd made it without getting wet. He smiled, turned to the door, knocked, then rang the doorbell twice in case they hadn't heard.

A few seconds later the deadbolt slid back, the door opened a fraction, and a woman's eye looked out. "Can I help you?" she asked. She spoke as though drowsy or confused—Lou couldn't quite decide which.

"I was wonderin if Jason was home," he said.

"Um . . . Jason? Jason is . . . It's very early."

"He told me to stop by."

"He . . . he did?" The woman blinked a few times, then looked at Lou again as though reassessing him. "You're the boy that just moved in, aren't you?"

"Lou Coldwell," he said, nodding.

"So you are a Coldwell," Nancy said, as though things suddenly made sense to her.

"Right," said Lou, a bit unsure. "My dad's Paul."

"Well, Lou Coldwell, I'm Nancy Chang." She opened the door a little wider and with her hand swept a strand of damp hair from her forehead and tucked it behind her ears. She wore a blue terrycloth robe cinched at the waist, held closed at the neck with her hand. "Jason asked you to come over at this time?"

Lou understood now. He looked away, back across the street at his own house, and spoke quietly. "I'm sorry, ma'am. I waited for your light to turn on. I thought you all was up."

Nancy's head tipped to one side. She looked down at Lou and rubbed the back of her neck. A smile slowly lit her face. "That was very considerate of you, Lou, but Jason is still asleep."

"Will you just tell him I came by and he can come over and get me anytime he's not busy?"

"Sure, but I'm just a little confused here—how did you meet Jason?"

"He came by yesterday and said he was going to take me . . . um, just to this old trail he knows."

"Jason said that?"

"Yeah. But he said he had a real busy schedule so I should just come by and try to catch him. I figured this morning before he left for work would be best."

"A busy schedule, huh?" Nancy thought a moment, then laughed quietly. "It's funny, Lou, but I think Jason's schedule has opened up. A few last-minute cancellations. You're more than welcome to come in and wait for him."

"You sure?"

"He wouldn't have it any other way. Now have you had breakfast yet?"

Lou explained that all they had was Shredded Wheat, which he liked almost as much as shoe leather, so Nancy brought him inside and let him watch TV in the living room while she dressed and fixed her hair. Then she made a breakfast of a ham-and-cheese omelettes and sliced fruit. While they ate, she asked Lou about his father, their past, and their plans in Esperanza. Speaking in hazy generalizations, Lou revealed little more than the obvious.

"Do you and your dad ever see Paul's uncle anymore?" Seeing the question on Lou's face, Nancy added, "I've lived here a long time. I knew your father when he was your age, back before . . . back before your uncle had to take him in."

"Uncle Melvin's around," said Lou. He seemed a little uncomfortable with the subject, so Nancy quickly asked him what Paul had done since then.

Lou thought, took a sip of his juice, then said proudly, "Well, when he was nineteen, he started as a semi-professional boxer on the western circuit. Did all right, too. Eleven wins and one loss. Then he met my mom and she had me and he had to quit."

Nancy was debating whether to ask what had happened to Lou's mom when Jason walked into the kitchen.

"Who're you talking to?" he asked. Then he saw Lou.

"Hey, Jason," Lou called, his mouth full of fruit.

"Lou came by this morning, said you'd offered to take him up to some trail." Nancy smiled. "I figured since your ever-busy schedule had miraculously cleared, it must've been meant for today."

Jason looked at Nancy, at Lou, back at Nancy.

"You did tell him you'd take him, didn't you?" said Nancy.

Jason sighed, slid his palm over his face, and sat at the table across from Lou. "Right," he said. "The trail."

Lou smiled at Jason, shoveled in a bite of omelet, and said, mouth full, "This is gonna be awesome."

■ ■ ■

After breakfast, Jason strapped his knee brace over his jeans, and met Lou in the front yard. The sun had risen now and though it was not yet nine o'clock, the air was hot and dry and bits of cotton from the cottonwoods down the street floated past on the morning breeze. Across the street the Coldwells' maple had been pruned, its dead branches now piled beneath the tree. Though lopsided, the tree looked like it had a fighting chance of survival now.

"You guys do all that last night?" asked Jason.

Lou nodded.

"I'm impressed." Jason pulled on a baseball cap and turned to Lou. "You ready?"

"Just got to grab a few tools."

The dry stubble of weeds crunched beneath their shoes as they walked to the Coldwells' front door. Lou kicked it open and let Jason in. It was the smell Jason noticed first—a dank acrid smell that reminded him of decay and mold.

"I think they're back in my dad's room," said Lou. "I'll just be a sec."

He disappeared down the narrow hall into one of the bedrooms. Trying not to breathe deeply, Jason stood in the entryway and looked over the house. He noticed first the absence of all carpets: they'd been torn out, though most of the tack strips still remained. The walls were made from the wood-paneling that had been popular twenty or thirty years back, but now the dark finish merely drew in what little light the single bulb could manage. From where he stood, Jason could see into part of the living room, where there also was no carpet, nor even any furniture, but instead only a stack of flattened cardboard boxes and an old vinyl chair parked in front of the window.

The only real sign that people lived there came in the form of a single picture frame mounted on the wall, which, because it was the only ornament, drew the eye almost magnetically. It was a picture of a younger Lou, perhaps ten, sitting beside Paul, who wore a white shirt with a collar that seemed too tight for his thick neck and a crooked tie. Paul's smile, though sincere, seemed awkward, as though some deep worry had surfaced in his mind the moment before the camera shutter had snapped. Jason stepped closer and saw that Paul's left arm stretched unnaturally across his body, the hand resting over the right knee of his jeans. His right arm lay over Lou's thin shoulders. Jason wondered why the photographer had posed Paul that way, but then he noticed the wear in the denim around the knee and the white spot that showed between Paul's finger and thumb: he'd been covering a hole in his jeans.

Seeing the small picture—Paul's awkward smile, the hole at the knee—and the house in which he and his son now lived, Jason saw clearly enough that their life to this point had been one of poverty and struggle, and that after all the long years it had still brought them back to a run-down house and a grunt-level job at a copper mine. He couldn't help but wonder what their story was and why the roads of some lives were paved with ease and luxury, while others wandered with only the roughest of trails to follow. He thought of the naked children playing in the streets of Narang, he thought of Erika and her two daughters, he thought of his mother, nearly twenty years earlier, seeing the black smoke billow from the mine warehouse across the valley and hearing the phone ring.

The weight grew within him until at last he shouted down the hallway, "I'll be outside, Lou," and quickly stepped out into the sunlight and breathed in the fresh air. Lou came out a short time later, a small toolbox in hand, and they set off down the street. Jason felt at once glad to be leaving the house, foolish for letting his emotions affect him so.

■ ■ ■

They walked without speaking down Prospector Street to the chainlink fence, then followed it to the willow in the Martins' yard. *It doesn't look anything like a mushroom,* Lou thought as they walked into its shade.

Jason went to a small rise where the willow's roots had pushed up the fence. Lou slid the toolbox under, then squirmed through on his belly. Jason looked down the street one last time and mumbled some-thing and then got down on his belly and tried to wriggle under, but one of the fence-links caught the back of his pants and held him pinned, face-down on the ground. Jason grunted, pulled at weeds with his hands, tried to kick free with his legs. The harder he tried, the sillier he looked.

"A little help here," he gasped finally, his face pressed into a thick growth of dandelions.

Lou stood by, trying not to laugh, but the urge was too strong and it surged up through his nose with a great snort.

"Are you laughing?" asked Jason.

"No," said Lou, although he clearly was.

"You are laughing."

"Well it ain't my fault. You look dumber than a bag of lead bricks."

"Nice. After you're done insulting me maybe you could unhook me."

Lou went over and pulled the fence back.

"If only the neighbors could see me now," Jason grunted, pulling the lower half of his body through.

"Why didn't you just climb over it?" asked Lou.

Jason stood, brushed off his clothes, and looked at the fence as though seeing it for the first time. "I don't know," he said finally. "We just always did it that way when we were kids."

"You're a little bigger than you were."

Jason sighed, turned away from the fence. "Next time maybe you could make your suggestions *before* I make an idiot of myself."

"I'll do my best," said Lou. He was looking at Jason's face and once again trying not to laugh.

"What?" asked Jason.

"You got a little dandelion stuck over your ear."

Jason felt for it with his hand, pulled it out, looked at it. A full bright yellow bud, broken at the stalk.

"Flowers are a good look for you," said Lou. "Puts me in a mood to hula."

"I'm going to put you in different mood here in a second."

Jason, also laughing now, threw down the dandelion and stomped it under his shoe. "Let's get out of here before the Martin lady sees us. She was mean when I was a kid and the years haven't been kind to her."

The trail turned out to be better marked than Jason had expected, and he assumed the deer that often came down into the valley must've kept it fresh. His knee ached from the exertion of the hike and his out-of-shape muscles burned, but it felt good to be outside. Jason leading, they followed a long curve along the base of the mountain, through groves of scrub oak, until at last they came to a steep gully.

The creek ran at the bottom of the gully and was shrinking fast now that the spring runoff had come and gone. Grabbing at roots to steady themselves on the loose earth, they slid down and turned upstream and walked in silence along the rocks at the edge of the water. A short time later they seemed to cross some hidden line: the scrub oak quit suddenly and they walked among white aspens, the breeze shivering the leaves above, the creek covered over like a tunnel by the high branches. A little way ahead through breaks in the canopy they could now see the limestone bluffs over Fire Creek.

"Sure is nice up here," said Lou as they walked. "I can see why my dad would've liked this place."

"How old was your dad when he moved from here?"

"About my age, I guess. His mom and dad died and he had to live with his uncle."

A flock of quail, startled from the brush by the heavy footfalls, scattered into the trees. For a time Jason and Lou could hear their strange clucking from the undergrowth around them.

"So what brought you guys back here now?" asked Jason.

"I just woke up one day and my dad said he'd quit his job down at Kent's Auto and we was movin out of the motel in Kanab."

"You lived in a motel?"

Lou walked in silence for a time, and his face was troubled, as though he were weighing out possible answers and had not yet discovered one he liked. "Uncle Melvin owned the motel," he said at last. "My dad moved us there about three months ago. Said he needed to save money fast. Anyway, after a month or so Melvin raised the rent, which is why we're here now."

"This the same uncle that took your dad in when he was a kid?"

"Same one."

"Sounds like a nice guy."

"He's the only real family we got."

Jason glanced back. The boy's glasses shone with reflected sunlight and his face offered no hint of whether he was bitter about it or not. Once again they walked in silence, and Jason's thoughts turned to Paul himself. Remembering the "For Sale" sign on the truck, he couldn't help but wonder why Paul needed to save money fast, as Lou had put it. He decided to probe a little further.

"So how's your dad like it at Esperanza Copper?"

"All right, I guess. I don't think he likes the early mornings, though. He's been getting headaches in the morning lately. A lot of times he gets so sick he throws up."

"How come?"

Lou hesitated, just long enough to make Jason wonder if he was hiding something. "Stress, maybe," he said finally.

They came through the trees to Fire Creek, to its broken picnic tables and weedy firepits. The clearing was quiet and still, sunlight bright on the shallow creek, and it wasn't hard to imagine they'd stumbled onto the ruins of some ancient culture. Below them about fifty yards, the dirt road—two tracks with cheatgrass growing between—looped up toward them and then turned and followed the canyon away into the trees.

"You know why they call it Fire Creek?" Lou asked, as they stood taking in the view.

"Someone told me it was because right after the first people settled the valley, a lightning strike set this whole canyon burning. For a few days the creekwater ran dark with ash."

"Doesn't look like there was any fire," said Lou, looking at the trees and wild grasses.

"Time can fix a lot of things," said Jason, shrugging.

They left the picnic grounds and climbed into the pine grove, passing by the tree scarred with lovers' names. The fort was suddenly before them, its broken walls and collapsed roof lying just as Lou had left them, the prints of his high-tops still marking the dry earth around it.

"This is what my dad built," said Lou proudly, as though seeing the fort as it had been and not as it was now.

"It's something, all right," said Jason. He walked to the structure and looked closely at the walls. The wood was dark and rotten where it touched the ground, dry and crumbling on the top side.

"I brought nails and a hammer and woodscrews and a screwdriver set," said Lou, tossing down the small toolbox.

"This wood's not going to work."

"Why not?"

"Too old."

"I can make it work," Lou said hopefully.

"That wood'll crumble the moment a nail touches it."

Lou rubbed his hand over it, then thumped it with his knuckles, making a soft dead sound.

"I guess I'll have to haul up some new wood," he said.

"There's no way. It's too far."

"You got any better ideas?"

Jason turned and looked down toward the tables hidden behind the trees. "I think I do," he said.

That afternoon, piece by piece, the old outhouses on the far side of the picnic grounds came down. There was no smell to distract them, since the toilets had been removed and the pits filled in with dirt when the place had been abandoned. And once they stripped the aluminum siding from the walls with the claw of the hammer, working as quietly as they could to avoid attracting attention, they found that the wood was in surprisingly good condition. The sun beat over them, sweat stains spread across Jason's hat, and he said often that it was stupid not to bring any water, yet to his surprise he found that he enjoyed the heat and the work and the air flavored with pinesap and aspen and the scenery he'd not known in years. He felt better than he had in a long time, better than he had since Rodney died.

As they worked, Jason questioned Lou further about his past and his father. For his part, Lou seemed reluctant to speak about it, though he did explain proudly, as he had earlier that day to Nancy, that Paul had once been a semi-professional boxer.

"He loves boxing," Lou said, as he worked to separate a stubborn two-by-four from the flat pressboard walls. "He's even entered some local tournament down at a place called Fat Smithy's or something."

"Fat Sammy's," said Jason. He'd taken a seat against a nearby boulder to rest his knee.

"You know about it?"

"I'll be working it, setting up the bleachers and stuff and probably doing some vending."

"You gonna watch the fights?"

"Maybe."

"You should watch my dad fight. He's got this incredible right hook. Just comes out of nowhere and blows people away."

Jason sat there with his leg stretched out before him and watched Lou struggle with the pressboard.

"So why's your dad selling his truck?" he asked, turning the conversation back to his unanswered questions from earlier that afternoon.

"What?" said Lou.

"Your dad's truck—how come he wants to sell it?"

Throwing his weight back on the hammer to pry off the two-by-four, Lou grunted something about a savings account, and then the board gave suddenly and he fell back onto the seat of his pants.

"You all right?" asked Jason.

Lou answered the question by putting aside the pressboard, then standing, grabbing the two-by-four, and flinging it away. It cartwheeled down the steep hill and slammed up against one of the old tables.

"Did you say something about a savings account?" asked Jason.

"Yeah. He's trying to save money."

They were back where they'd started, Jason realized with a sigh. "What I mean is why does he need money so fast?"

Annoyed and embarrassed by his fall, Lou shot Jason an exasperated look. "Can we talk about something else for a while?"

"Sure," said Jason. "No problem."

And though they spoke of other things while they finished dismantling the outhouses and hauling the wood up to the fort, Jason couldn't help but wonder why Lou hadn't answered the question. The matter grew in his mind as they walked back from the canyon and jumped the fence near the Martins' willow and made their way back to Hollow Stone Drive. In the street between their houses, when Jason said goodbye to Lou and wished him luck on the fort—"If you get caught, don't tell them I took you up there," he said, laughing— he couldn't help but notice again the old house and wonder what had brought Paul suddenly back.

After Lou had gone inside, Jason went into the backyard and sat on one of the patio chairs and looked up at the peaks above Fire

Creek. The world had enough problems; it hardly needed Paul and Lou's. Jason wondered, if only for a small moment, if God had brought him back to help Lou and Paul. But the thought was ridiculous. He was trying, like some self-righteous zealot, to make himself the hero of someone else's story. He opened his book to the bookmark and tried to put the thought out of his mind. For a time, he even succeeded.

CHAPTER 11

A few days later, on July 14, Paul sold his truck. Jason knew because in the late afternoon, as he sat reading on the front porch, he saw his neighbor pedaling home on a ten-speed whose frame looked too battered to function. A gray plastic lunchbox rattled in a basket behind the seat. When Paul saw Jason, he stopped at the curb and for a minute or two they chatted. Jason complimented him on the work he'd done in his yard.

"Plenty more yet to do," said Paul, pleased. "My old man used to keep this place lookin like a photo from one of those home magazines."

Jason wished him luck with his work and they said their goodbyes. As he watched Paul push his bike up the broken driveway, park it in the carport, and go inside, he regretted that he hadn't tried to find out if he'd been right to suspect that he had serious money problems. He sighed and reminded himself that they were, after all, neighbors and would see each other again.

■ ■ ■

Every morning over the next week, as Jason sat at the table in the kitchen eating his breakfast, he saw Lou set out for his day's work at fort. As though his movements were set by a clock's gears, he walked out the front door at 8:30 precisely, toolbox in hand, and headed away toward Prospector Street. Jason often worried, seeing him go, about what Paul would think when he found out where Lou went every day, and whether Lou would tell Paul about his own part in the plan.

On Friday evening Jason set his alarm and went to bed early. He had to be at Fat Sammy's the following morning at 7:00 to start setting up for the tournament. The alarm, however, proved unnecessary: he woke from another dream while it was still dark.

They'd been sitting by the wall again, Rodney and he, waiting for Austen's ride, when down the dirt road a short distance, a woman veiled in a black burka turned the corner and started toward them. But when she saw the soldiers sitting there, she spun back to run away, and as she turned, her veil lifted and Jason saw, or thought he saw, in that tiny moment, Alison's face beneath the dark fabric. And then she was gone, leaving Jason to stare after her and wonder what had just happened.

I think I'm losing my grip, he said at last, turning to Rod. But Rodney wasn't there; he'd stood and started walking away down the street in the other direction.

Where are you going? Jason called, trying to decide whether to risk standing and following.

Home.

You can't go home!

But Rodney wasn't listening. He took off his helmet and hurled it away into a pile of broken concrete and rubble, then unloaded his M-16 and tossed it into the gutter where the stagnant water and waste lay.

My girls are waiting for me! he shouted. He walked a few more steps before glancing back. You should go home too, Chang. There's nothing for you here anymore.

He walked on and didn't look back and Jason sat there watching him in frustration, wanting to follow but not daring the risk.

Jason lay in his bed for a long time, thinking it through, puzzling out various meanings, until through the open bedroom window he heard movement. He sat up and parted the blinds. Paul was pushing his bike down his drive, his lunchbox stowed in the basket behind the seat. At the curb he mounted and pedaled away toward the mine offices. Apparently, he worked Saturdays too.

Jason showered, dressed, and made himself a breakfast of eggs and a bagel. As he ate he flipped between cable news channels. Suicide bombing in the Middle East. Hollywood dietician. Young girl missing in Colorado. Big corporate accounting scandal defrauds thousands of their retirement plans and savings. They could just replay last month's news, thought Jason, and no one would notice the difference.

He turned off the tube and took Nancy's car keys (he'd made arrangements with her the previous day) and went out to the carport. It was only 6:30, so he drove slowly around town and looked out at the houses, nearly all of them quiet on a Saturday morning. He wondered about the people inside, what their stories were, how they'd landed in Esperanza. He wondered how many of them enjoyed their lives and how many were even now coping with personal loss or tragedy. He wondered how many no longer cared. He thought of Lou and Paul.

Twenty minutes later he pulled into the parking lot at Fat Sammy's.

■ ■ ■

In the late afternoon Paul pedaled from the mine offices and stopped by the sporting goods store on Center Street. He came out with a long thin package, which he tied with short ropes to the basket on his bike. When he got home, Lou was outside in the backyard cutting down weeds (his chore for the day), and didn't see him come in. Paul went back to Lou's room with the package, and then a short time later came out empty-handed to the backyard.

"Hey, Lou. Come in for a second. I got something to show you."

Lou pulled a weed and threw it onto the pile. "What is it?"

"Check your room."

Lou went down the hall to his bedroom, opened the door, switched on the light. Against the near wall, his mattress, the only furnishing in the room, lay flat on the floorboards, a quilt thrown over the top. Above the mattress, a poster of Mohammed Ali had been tacked to the wall. The boxer's eyes were dark and focused, his face strangely calm, his right hand swinging through George Foreman's chin. The drops of sweat flung off of Foreman's torqued face were frozen in midair, blurring the heads of several gaping spectators in the background. Lou smiled.

He found his father sitting on the front porch.

"What'd you think?" Paul asked.

"Awesome," said Lou. He paused, looked at his father. "But I thought we were tryin to save all our money."

"Your room looked bare." Paul squeezed his son's shoulder lightly and added, "Besides, I needed something to get me thinkin about the tournament."

"When's it start?"

"Friday. Runs every weekend after that till there's only one fighter left—me, of course."

"Your headaches gettin any better?"

Paul frowned and withdrew his hand. "I'm in plenty good shape for the kind of yahoos you'll get at a tournament like this. I bet none of these boys even know how to fight other than to just start swinging their fists like a windmill."

"You changed your mind about lettin me come?"

"No. It's no kind of place for a kid."

"Please. Just to your fight."

"We're not talkin about this again."

Lou sighed and looked away. "You sure you're goin to win?" he asked.

"I'll win," said Paul. "For two-thousand bucks, I'll win easy."

■ ■ ■

On Sunday, shortly after Nancy left for church, Lou crossed the street and knocked on the Changs' front door. He'd not seen Jason in the car with Nancy when she left, and he hoped now to talk to him in private. When Jason answered the door he looked a little surprised.

"What's up, Lou?"

Lou leaned around and looked past him into the house. "Your mom's at church, right?"

"Yeah. Why?"

"How come you didn't go?"

Jason thought for a time. "I guess I'm not ready to go back yet." Brows furrowed, he looked at Lou and quickly asked, "Is that what you came to ask me?"

"No. I came to ask if you're still workin at the boxing tournament?"

Jason nodded. "We started setting up yesterday."

"You goin to work the fight nights?"

"Probably. Why?"

"I need a favor."

"What kind of favor?"

"I need you to sneak me in to Fat Sammy's."

"What?"

"My dad won't let me go. This'll probably be the only chance I'll get to see him box."

"I can't do that."

"Why not? It's a big place isn't it?"

"For one thing, it's not *in* Fat Sammy's—it's *behind* it. Outside. For another thing, I agree with your dad, it's no place for a kid." Jason paused and an amused smile lit his face. "Just curious, but what in the world made you think I'd go for this?"

"You showed me how to sneak into Fire Creek."

"That was different."

"How?"

"Drunken men don't scream for blood at Fire Creek."

Clearly frustrated, Lou turned, looked back at his house, and seemed to be struggling to find some new argument to throw at Jason. In the end, he set reason aside and decided on a simpler tactic. "Come on, Jason," he begged. "My dad's gonna win this thing."

"Sorry, Lou. I can't."

Lou looked at Jason one last time and suddenly his demeanor changed: gone were the sagging shoulders, the frown, the disappointment. "It's fine," he said, smiling. "No big deal. I shouldn't have come over here in the first place. Just do me a favor and don't say anything to my dad."

"Sure," said Jason, wondering at the quick change.

Lou hopped down the porch steps and jogged back across the street. For a time Jason stood in the doorway, thinking, then he went into the kitchen and got the cordless and dialed.

"No one is available to take your call," spoke a deep, though somehow familiar voice. "Please leave a message."

"This is for Rooster," said Jason, after the beep. "It's Jason Chang. Give me a call, buddy. I need to ask you a favor for this weekend—"

"Jason!" Rooster interrupted. "What's up, bro?"

"Rooster?"

"You know it."

"I thought I was talking to the machine."

"Just me, dude." Rooster's voice dropped to that same slow bass: "No one is available to take your call. I am an answering machine. Beam me up, Scotty." He quit and the beep sounded once again.

"What is that?"

"Some stupid kid's robot toy I found. Sounds a lot like a machine beep, huh?" He beeped it several more times to make the point.

"You know you're crazy, right?"

"Just screening my calls, bro. You never know who's got your number these days, what with the Internet and all. Did you know there are secret databases out there with everything from your eye color to your favorite food to the names of your old girlfriends? Just right out there where anyone can get at them."

"It's a scary world," said Jason. He asked Rooster if he and his family were still holding their annual Pioneer Day fireworks show in front of their house. Rooster said they were—"at nine o'clock of the p.m.," his exact words.

"Good. I need you to invite someone for me."

"Sure. No prob."

"It's this kid that lives across from me."

"Lou Coldwell."

"You've met them?"

"No. But I did some checking."

"Right. Of course you did. Anyway, I think he might try to sneak down to watch his dad—"

"Paul."

"Right—watch *Paul* box in Sammy's tournament." Jason went on to explain his conversation with Lou a few minutes earlier and how he worried about what might happen if Paul discovered the boy at the tournament. Since it opened on Pioneer Day, Jason asked Rooster to invite Lou to the fireworks show and keep an eye on him.

"No prob," said Rooster. "I'll run the invite through the old man so the kid can't shoot me down."

"Now you're thinking."

"Watch for me, dude. I'll be by in three minutes."

"Thanks, bro."

"No biggie. Over and out."

Rooster hung up and as promised, three minutes later, Jason, watching from the living room window, saw him walk to the Coldwells' front door and knock. Paul answered and they exchanged a few words, then Paul called Lou to the door. Rooster spoke for a time to the boy and made several quick explosive gestures with his hands. Lou seemed not at all happy with what he was saying. Paul, on the other hand, smiled and clapped his son on the back, and spoke excitedly to him. They both shook Rooster's hand before saying goodbye and shutting the door.

Rooster then walked out to the sidewalk, took up an imaginary rifle, aimed it at the window where Jason sat, and fired several rounds. Then he laughed, made the all clear sign, and walked back down the street.

CHAPTER 12

On Friday evening Jason parked his mother's Buick in the overcrowded lot beneath a sign that read *Fat Sammy's Bar and Restaurant* and featured a cartoonish fat man with a beer mug, pinpricks of brown for eyes, and cheeks like red balloons. The paint on the sign, once bright and friendly, had weathered away from the cartoon man's double chin, revealing the dark knots and lines of the wood beneath. The wide front windows of the restaurant itself were lettered with heavy brush strokes:

It's BA-A-A-C-K
Esperanza Annual Boxing Tournament!!!
Friday Nites Starting Pioneer Day!!!!

Jason stood outside the windows, looking into the restaurant. Inside, wearing a white half-apron and a black Sammy's shirt, Alison stood at a table, taking orders from a family of four. Busy with her notes, she didn't notice him, and so Jason watched her until at last she put away her pad, collected the menus, and started toward the kitchen.

But then she stopped and as though she sensed him standing there, turned to look at him. For a moment neither of them moved and a silent question passed between them, each wondering what the other would do, what the other was thinking—until at last Alison turned away, walked quickly back into the kitchen like she'd never seen him at all.

It hurt, more than Jason thought it would, and for a while he just stood there staring dumbly until the couple eating at the table closest to the window started shooting him annoyed looks.

Reluctantly, he walked away, intending to go around to the back of the restaurant, where the tournament was about to begin. But Alison's call stopped him. He looked back. She was walking out the double-doors toward him.

"Hi," he said lamely.

She stopped several feet away, folded her arms, and considered him with an expression just as well suited for a stranger. "What are you doing here?"

"Going to the tournament."

"You're actually going to watch it?"

"I'm working. It's a job—Rooster signed me up for it."

She looked away at the town, the high trees gently stirring in the falling light, the clouds flushed above Fire Creek.

"Why didn't you call me?" she asked finally.

"I did. I mean I tried to."

"What's that supposed to mean?"

"I don't know. I'm sorry."

They stood in front of the restaurant, Alison still refusing to look at him.

"I've been reading the book you sent me."

"Great."

"It's good."

"I've got to get back to work."

"Okay."

"So that's it then? Just 'okay?'"

"What do you want me to say?"

"I don't know."

Alison glanced through the restaurant windows at her tables. "I've really got to go."

She started toward the door, then stopped and looked back at Jason.

"Are we done?"

Jason knew what she meant. "I hope not," he said.

Alison nodded and for a moment Jason thought she might walk back out to him. But instead she just sighed and said, "I'll be around," and then she was gone.

Following a path tramped into the weeds alongside the restaurant's dirty cinderblock wall, Jason walked slowly around to the back. He could hear music now—the biting blues of an old Muddy Waters tune—all distorted and tinny on an overworked speaker system, which they'd rigged early that week. He came around the corner to a dry grassy field, over which they'd set up three rickety wood bleachers, each eight rows high and already laden with rugged-looking spectators, nearly all of them male. The bleachers bounded the makeshift boxing ring—tattered green gym mats they'd borrowed from the high school and thrown down over a raised wood stage. Four thick elastic ropes anchored to padded poles in the corners completed the structure.

At each end of the makeshift arena, a metal pole anchored to a cement-filled tire stood with a pair of floodlights rigged to the top. Behind the bleachers and the ring, a weedy field stretched away in the fading light, and along the near side of it, hiding an irrigation ditch, ran a straight row of dark gnarled trees. At their closest point, these trees came within forty feet of the bleachers. Between the trees and the bleachers sat a rusted-out pickup with no tires and a windshield cracked like a spider web and a row of five orange porta-potties.

It had taken four workers, Jason included, three full days to set up everything, but as he looked it over now he felt only a sense of waste. He'd been to the tournament once before he'd joined the Marines; he knew the type of men it drew from Esperanza and the surrounding towns and what they all hoped to see.

He looked toward the ring. The top rope had gone slack and three men worked to tighten it, two of them gripping it with both hands and struggling to pull it taut, their boots skidding over the dirt. The other man—rod-thin and gray-haired, dressed in jeans and a flannel shirt rolled up around his hairy forearms—was Sammy Manchester himself, restaurant owner and tournament sponsor. He was jerking a wrench around at one of the corner posts to tighten the clamp bolt. Jason walked to them.

"There," Sammy said, standing back and tapping the bolt with his wrench. "That ought to hold her."

One of his helpers pulled the rope back to test its resistance and let it snap back into place.

"How's it going, boys?" Jason said, walking over to them.

"Well if it isn't Jason Ching-Chang-Chong-along," said Sammy happily. He put his wrench on the mat and extended a hand. The fingers and nails were smudged with grease. Jason shook it.

"Hey, Sammy," one of the helpers said. "We're gonna go grab our seats before someone else does."

"Thanks, boys," Sammy said. "Enjoy the fights."

The two men walked away.

"So what do you think, Jason?" Sammy asked, looking over the set-up.

"I think you already got more spectators here than ever and the fights don't even start for another twenty minutes."

"And every ugly mug you see means five bucks in my pocket, plus another buck for every beer—and some of these boys can drink their body weight."

"Great for you," said Jason dryly. "So we all set?"

"Everything's up to snuff. Good old Carlos Alvarez should be here any second and then we can get this shindig started."

"Carlos who?"

"Alvarez. The fight doc. Truth be told, a gynecologist, but he don't want that publicized around here if you know what I mean." Sammy laughed hoarsely, then sighed. "Carlos is troopin out from Payson. Had to pay out a hundred-and-fifty bucks plus gas to get him out here."

"I didn't know you hired a doctor."

"Some of the legal eagles gave me a hard time."

"So you still want me on drinks tonight?"

"Well there's a little bit of an issue there," said Sammy, scratching his head.

"Yeah?"

"Had a little change of heart, Jason. Now you're a handsome guy and all, but I got to thinkin I might could sell more beer if I had a few ladies mannin—I mean, womanin—the kegs."

Jason looked at Sammy. "So what? You just change it just like that?"

Sammy shrugged. "Business is business, Chang. You know that."

"You could've at least called me."

"Tell you what I'm goin to do," said Sammy, smiling again. He slapped Jason on the shoulder, making him flinch. "I'm gonna give you a free seat and all the beer you can drink for the rest of the tournament."

"You already gave me a free seat, and I don't drink."

Before Sammy could respond, the men seated or milling around the bleachers let out a raucous cheer. Following the direction of their gaze, Jason turned and watched four waitresses in short black skirts and red Sammy's T-shirts cart two silver kegs out the back door of the restaurant. "You got to admit they look better in skirts than you do, Chang," said Sammy, slapping Jason on the back again.

"The circus has come to town," Jason said, mostly to himself.

"Come on, buddy," said Sammy, laughing. "Where's your patriotic fervor? This is capitalism hard at work in our own humble community. This is what you was fightin for out there in Afghanistan."

Jason turned suddenly cold. He looked hard at Sammy and said in a low voice, "You don't have a clue what I was fighting for."

"Sorry, buddy," said Sammy, raising his hands. "Didn't mean to touch a nerve."

Jason turned away, shook his head. "Just tell me what time Paul Coldwell fights and I'm out of your hair," he said.

"Friend of yours?" Sammy asked, pulling a card out of his pocket and looking at it.

"Neighbor."

"Final match," Sammy said. He put the card back into his pocket.

"How many are there?"

"Eight. I let in sixteen fighters this year. Keeps it nice and tidy for the tournament."

Jason walked away without another word. He cut through the men walking toward the beer to the back wall of the restaurant, where he leaned back, folded his arms, and watched as the crowd grew around the waitresses and the kegs.

■ ■ ■

Yellow light from two porch lamps washed Rooster Montgomery's yard and the near side of the house. Lou sat at the far end of a row of folding chairs next to Rooster, who was fiddling with the knobs and switches of a battery-powered boom box. In the other chairs sat a row of six dark-haired children, siblings by the look of them, hands folded in their laps.

Lou leaned toward Rooster and whispered, "What's with your family?"

"What do you mean?" asked Rooster.

"They look like they're at a funeral."

Rooster shrugged. "My dad believes in establishing a house of order."

"I guess you'd have to with seven kids."

"Seven?"

"Yeah. You plus the six of them."

"Oh. There's actually eleven of us. I got a brother away at scout camp, a brother and sister away at college, and my youngest sister's still inside."

"Ten brother and sisters," said Lou, shaking his head.

"It's all right," said Rooster, again tinkering with the boombox. "Being the oldest I get to keep them in line."

Behind them, Rooster's father—a heavyset, serious-looking man with wire-rim glasses came out of the house, carrying a large plastic bucket filled with fireworks of all colors and sizes. Rooster's mother, a short round-faced woman with long hair wrapped up like a cinnamon bun, followed closely behind. The father walked heavily out to the curb and thumped the bucket down on the road.

"Get ready to light em, Abednego," he said angrily, before spinning around, stepping past Rooster's mother, and heading back toward the house.

Rooster's mother stood by the other children and looked after him. "She's just a little scared," she called, pleading with him.

"Scared," he repeated, waving his hands over his head, keeping his quick pace. "She should've thought of that before she begged me to buy the most expensive fireworks."

Lou watched as he walked back into the house and slammed the door. He looked to Rooster for an explanation.

"My little sister's afraid of everything." Rooster emptied the batteries out of the boombox and turned them around. "My dad always makes her face her fears, but it only makes things worse." The boom box came suddenly to life in Rooster's hands, hissing with static. "Fixed," he announced and passed it down the row to his mother.

"Thank you, Abednego," his mother said. She plugged in a tape and hit play and suddenly a full brass band was blaring out 'You're a Grand Ol' Flag.'"

"I know Pioneer Day is just a Utah holiday," she said, turning to Lou, "but I just can't enjoy fireworks without a little patriotic music."

Behind them, the front door again opened and Lou looked back to see Rooster's father emerge, a young girl's tiny hand gripped within his own.

"I don't want to!" the girl screamed.

"Yes you do, Katie. It's all in your head." He kicked the door shut and dragged Katie toward the folding chairs.

"No," Katie said, struggling against her father's grip. Too loud."

"So cover your ears," Rooster's father barked. "This is family time."

He took Katie beneath the arms and plopped her down on her mother's lap. She looked up through the dark hair that had fallen over her eyes and shouted, "Fireworks suck!"

Rooster's father stiffened as though he'd been shot, Rooster's mother gasped, and for a few seconds the entire family seemed to have been struck dumb. Rooster's father took a deep breath and leveled his gaze on his wife. He spoke slowly, as though holding back only with great effort some internal pressure. "Has she been watching television again?"

Rooster's mother cradled Katie's head into her blouse, stroked her hair, and looked defiantly up at her husband. "We'll talk about this later," she said.

After a moment of hesitation Rooster's father suddenly turned his attention to the other children. "We're going to have fun!" he shouted angrily. "Abednego! Fireworks! Now!"

"I'm up," Rooster whispered to Lou. He stood and walked out to the curb and the plastic bucket of fireworks.

"Eighty bucks," Rooster's father shouted, still looking at his children. "This *will* be fun. Got it?"

The children nodded as one. Lou slouched back in his chair and waited glumly for the show to begin.

■ ■ ■

Some twenty feet away from the bleachers and the other men, Jason sat on an old bar stool and stared toward the boxing ring, where the lights held off the thickening darkness. In the near corner sat a wiry man with a flattop and pallid skin that glistened with sweat in the stark light. His eyebrow had been cut badly, and Carlos Alvarez, an old but fit man with thinning black hair, stood over him and soaked the blood away with a white rag. The fighter raised a glove and wiped away a trickle of mixed sweat and blood from his eye.

At the other side of the ring a tall Polynesian with healthy brown skin and dark curls that grew long and thick stood leaning against the corner pole. His left arm was tattooed around the biceps with a thick weaving band and across his broad back ran three black Chinese characters. With no apparent wounds, he looked strong, calm, and confident.

Sammy, holding a styrofoam cup carefully in one hand, walked over and sat down on a stool next to Jason. A blast from an air horn started the next round.

"Don't look too good for Chapman," Sammy said. "Kawika's too strong."

Jason nodded. "Someone ought to throw in the towel before Chapman gets his clock cleaned."

It was too late. Kawika charged wildly out of his corner and without any respect for a possible counterpunch, launched a two punch combination of his own: a left that flashed across Chapman's chin, a right that buried itself in Chapman's stomach and doubled him over. Chapman came down hard, knees hitting first, his face slapping against the green mat. As the spectators shouted and jeered, he lay there with black mouthpiece hanging out between his lips, eyes shut tightly with pain.

Sammy jumped to his feet, his beer sloshing out of his cup. "Man, what a punch! Did you see that punch?"

"I saw it," said Jason, standing up and looking intently at Chapman. As he watched, Carlos Alvarez climbed through the ropes, knelt over Chapman, and talked into his ear. Meanwhile, the referee, a short man with a Fat Sammy's T-shirt and a belly that slopped over his belt, raised Kawika's arm.

"This is some way to celebrate the holiday," Sammy said happily.

"Just great," said Jason. If not for Paul's fight later on that evening, he would've been home by now. He checked his watch. 10:05. And still three more fights to go before Paul was up.

In the ring Chapman rose to a knee, his arm over Carlos's shoulder. Behind him, Kawika slipped through the ropes and jumped down from the wood stage.

"Come on, Chang," Sammy chided. "This beats the heck out of the usual fireworks shows."

Jason could only shake his head.

■ ■ ■

As Lou and the rest of the Montgomery family watched, Rooster took out a box of sparklers and a lighter. "It's not the Fourth of July, Mom," he said. "Can we cut the corny music now?"

"The music stays on," said his mother, and the brass band moved into the final refrain from "Stars and Stripes Forever." Rooster sighed and flicked the lighter until the fire caught. He held it to the first sparkler.

"Here we go, guys!" he said as it flared to life. "Come and get em! We got enough here to keep us going at least an hour or so."

Holding the lit sparkler aside, Rooster tried to work another out of the box with his free hand, but the lit sparkler slipped and brushed against his forearm. He shouted, jerked his arm back, and dropped the sparkler. A cascade of light, it tumbled down, hit against the rim of the bucket, and bounced in. For a quick moment, Rooster stood there gripping his burned arm, not noticing where it had fallen.

"Abednego!" his father shouted, rising to his feet. But it was too late. Blue sparks spouted from a cone at the top of the bucket and sprayed almost horizontally out over the curb. Rooster jumped forward, tried to snatch the lit sparkler from the bucket with quick snake-like strikes of his hands, but the biting sparks spraying from the cone kept him back. Then, suddenly, two more fireworks lit, and everything was chaos.

Rooster beat a quick retreat, his face hidden behind his arm, while sparks of all colors and varieties—some fizzing, some hissing, some popping—rained down over him and the street at strange angles. The light streaming from the bucket itself was intense. The Piccolo Petes began to shriek and a couple of Flaming Roses bounced and buzzed out of the box and down into the sloping gutter. The sides of the plastic bucket beaded, then began to sag and turn black and stringy. For perhaps fifteen seconds Lou and the others sat dumbfounded, their eyes reflecting the flares, their faces chameleon in the light—until the proud Chinese Pagoda, the largest firework of the bunch, simply exploded. A dull thump, a few startled screams from Rooster's mother and his sisters, and that was it.

Charred and toppled fireworks, some of them still sputtering a little, lay strewn around the melted remains of the bucket. Rooster stood at the curb, dumbstruck, his arms limp at his sides, as the brass band started into "Hail to the Chief."

Still sitting on her mother's lap, Katie began to laugh, softly at first, but louder as her mother grabbed her and whispered in her ear, trying desperately to quiet her. "Again!" shouted little Katie, pushing her mother's hands away. "Again! Again!"

To this point, Lou had done well to restrain himself, but now with Katie shouting for more and Rooster standing stunned in the gutter and the last of the fireworks sputtering in the street, he couldn't hold back any longer. A quick burst of laughter. He looked over at Rooster and his family and, laughed even harder, and tried to apologize: "I'm sorry," he wheezed, "but that's the funniest thing I've ever seen."

The rest of the family began to laugh, uneasily at first, but soon they were howling. At last, Rooster's father stood and clapped Rooster on the shoulder and said proudly, "Best eighty bucks I ever spent."

■ ■ ■

A few minutes later Rooster and his father went inside and got pushbrooms to clean up the street, while the kids folded up the chairs and took them inside. When Rooster came back out, Lou had gone. He looked down the street, but it was fully dark now and he couldn't see much of anything beyond the next yard.

"Any of you see where Lou got to?" Rooster asked his family.

They said they hadn't and seemed surprised to notice he had gone.

"Probably went home," said Rooster's father.

Rooster glanced at his watch. "Only ten o'clock," he muttered.

"What's a matter?" his father asked.

"The fireworks were supposed to go longer."

"Is there a problem?"

Rooster shook his head. "I hope not," he said.

■ ■ ■

It was nearly 11:00 before the last fight was ready to begin. The previous fights, with the exception of Kawika's quick dismissal of Chapman, had been predictable—men swinging wildly and without discipline, trying to knock each other out with haymakers. The fighters had fallen more often due to fatigue or loss of balance after a wild punch than to anything their opponents had done directly. But the men in the bleachers didn't care. They heckled the fighters whenever the pace slowed and threw papers cups and other bits of garbage into the ring if a fighter became too defensive. Eventually, owing more to luck than to skill, six other fighters followed Kawika into the second round, with Paul's fight the only one still remaining to be decided.

As he had all night, Jason sat apart from the rest of the men on a bar stool against the restaurant wall. He watched now as Carlos Alvarez taped Paul's hands and helped him with his gloves. Paul wore no shirt and the muscles of his chest and back and stomach were strong and well-defined. Paul's opponent, a man whose name had been announced as Terry Bunker, already had his gloves on and now waited in the ring, sparring lightly with a friend to keep warm.

When Carlos finished lacing the gloves, Paul leaned forward and spoke closely to him—Jason couldn't make out the words. Whatever he said, however, seemed to bring surprise to Carlos's face. Paul added a few more words, after which Carlos shrugged and went over to Paul's backpack, which lay on the ground near the ring, and took out an orange sparring helmet—the kind amateur boxers are required to wear. The helmet's padding came low across the forehead, over the cheekbones, and around to the back of the skull. Two small ear holes preserved the fighter's hearing. Carlos pulled the helmet over Paul's head and strapped it tight in the back. In the ring Terry stopped sparring and looked down.

"He can't wear that," he complained, raising a glove toward Paul.

"I brought another one," said Paul calmly. "It's in my bag. You're welcome to it."

"I ain't wearin no sissy helmet," said Terry.

Paul shrugged. He patted Carlos on the back of the head to thank him and climbed up into the ring. Somewhere in the bleachers, a man yelled drunkenly, "I didn't pay to see no helmets!"

A number of other voices shouted agreements. Sammy, who'd been sitting at a folding table beside the man who watched the clock, stepped forward.

"What's this about a helmet, Carlos?"

"He asked me to put it on," Carlos said, shrugging.

"I got a head condition," said Paul without looking down at Sammy. He was now leaning against the ropes in one of the corners, the continued jeers from the crowd having no apparent effect on him.

"What kind of condition?" asked Sammy.

"Just a condition."

Sammy turned to Carlos for help, but the doc merely shrugged again.

"I ain't fightin without it," said Paul.

Sammy swore under his breath, then turned to Terry Bunker. "What do you got to say about it, Bunker?"

"Let him wear the sissy helmet," Terry said, stretching his neck from side to side. "I'll bloody him either way."

"I take it you don't want to wear the other one," said Sammy.

"I won't need it," Terry said.

"Your call," said Sammy. He walked back to the scorer's table, picked up a mic, and turned on the PA. "Coldwell's wearin the helmet. Bunker's turned his down. Now where in damnation did the referee get to?"

At the beer table the ref had been chatting with one of the waitresses. Now, hearing his name, he drained his papercup, threw it down, and waddled quickly back to the ring, his belly bouncing over his beltbuckle. He climbed up (Sammy had to push him from behind to help) and checked both fighters' gloves and then pronounced them ready to begin. At the scorer's table the timekeeper triggered a stopwatch and let out a blast from the air horn. The two fighters angled out of their corners.

Jason stood and moved closer to the ring, where he could see the fight better. For the first few seconds, the fighters circled tentatively, Paul holding his fists still in front of his chin, Terry shifting his fighting positions every second as though trying somehow to create confusion with unorthodox movements. Paul, however, seemed unfazed. He side-stepped a wild punch, and with a movement as precise as an arrow through a bullseye snapped Terry's chin back with a left jab. The rest of his body seemed not to move, and almost before Terry knew what had happened, Paul had returned his glove to a defensive position and nimbly taken a new angle of attack. Stunned, Terry backstepped, blinked a few times, then shook out his head and took up his shifting stance once more.

For the rest of the first round, this process repeated itself again and again. Terry's nose was bleeding by the second minute, and he'd dropped all pretense of any fighting style whatsoever and instead tried wild bull charges that resulted each time in jabs to the face and rights to the body. Though clearly enraged, he couldn't find a way to get close enough to land a punch. When the air horn ended the first round, it was clear to Jason and everyone else how the fight would end—that is, it was clear to everyone but Terry.

For nearly two more rounds he endured punch after punch, until at the end of the third, too hurt and exhausted to raise his hands in defense, he took three quick punches in succession, stumbled back into the corner, turned his bleeding face away and drooped in a daze against the ropes.

The crowd leaned forward as one in their seats, expecting the final punch. But it never came. Instead, Paul stepped back and turned to the referee, who to this point had been standing idly in the opposite corner, oohing and aahing Paul's punches with the rest of the drunken men.

"End the fight," Paul barked, the words slurred by his mouthpiece.

"What?" said the referee, confused.

"End the fight!"

The referee looked at Terry still reeling and half-blind on the ropes, then reluctantly stepped forward and waved his hands over his heads. "Fight's over!" he shouted. "Coldwell takes it!"

Without acknowledging the men who now cheered him, Paul climbed down through the ropes and walked away from the ring.

CHAPTER 13

*M*ost of the men had gone, but a few still lingered ringside in the fringes of the light, their faces and forms half-shadowed. A short man with a face like a racoon's threw off a two-punch combination, an awkward imitation of Kawika's moves, in the direction of his fat companion. The fat man flinched, then slapped him on the back of the head and took a drag on his cigarette, the glow coloring his face warmly as he turned away from the light.

Jason sat a short distance away on the second row of the bleachers, listening absently to the murmur of their conversations and the bray of their laughter. He slouched back against the bench behind him, propped himself up with his elbows, and looked up at the moths churning around the floodlights, hundreds drawn in from the night-gray field. Behind him, the dark tangled trees growing over the ditch stirred quietly in the breeze. On the opposite side of the ring, Sammy was rolling an empty keg to the back door of the restaurant. He saw Jason, waved, and shouted, "See you next Friday, Chang-a-lang."

Paul Coldwell walked over from the porta potties. His short coarse hair was clumped with dried sweat and he wore soft moccasins, a black hooded sweatshirt fraying around the neckline, and a backpack filled with his gear.

"Thanks for waitin," he said.

Jason stood and the bleachers creaked beneath him. "No problem," he said.

As they walked past the boxing ring, the man with the raccoon face looked at Paul.

"Nice fight, Coldwell," he said.

"Yeah," echoed the fat man. "My money's on you next week."

Paul nodded to them. He and Jason walked on.

"Thanks for givin me a ride," Paul said quietly, as they rounded the corner of the restaurant and left the ring behind. "I could've biked if I had to, but I'm already gonna be sore enough."

"Doesn't seem like it. That Bunker guy never even landed a solid punch."

"But he sure took a lot of mine. Ten years ago he wouldn't of lasted thirty seconds."

"You must've been pretty good."

"I like to think even the worst of us gets at least one talent. I guess boxing's mine."

They stopped at the bike rack and Paul unlocked his ten-speed, and then they went on to the parking lot.

"That's quite a bike," said Jason.

"Had it for fifteen years," Paul said, pushing it along.

They set the bike in the Buick's trunk and drove away from the restaurant. The Esperanza streets were dark and still, the old trees shivering in the moonlight. It was quiet inside the car, the whir of the engine the only sound. They passed a church and Rooster's Market, both buildings well lit to keep away vandals and thieves. Jason rolled up his window, tapped his forefinger on the steering wheel, wished he could put away the lingering questions in his head. He sighed. There would never be a better chance.

"I ran into your son the other day," he said, trying to make it sound like any other random bit of conversation.

"Oh, yeah?"

"We talked a while." Jason hesitated, glanced at Paul. "He said he was a little worried about you."

He immediately regretted the blunt summary. He should've hinted at it, worked his way around the issue until Paul recognized it for himself. But too late now: Paul had turned his attention in from the quiet houses and was now looking directly at Jason. "What exactly did he say?" Paul asked, his tone measured, unnatural.

"Not much." Jason offered a quick casual smile. "Just something about you getting headaches a lot."

"I get a few every now and then," said Paul in that same measured tone. "But I'll tell Lou it's nothing to worry about."

"Are the headaches why you wore the helmet?"

Again, an overlong pause before the answer: "I always wear one if I can. Don't want to end up with a lisp." He smiled and forced an awkward laugh.

"I thought you said something about a head condition to Sammy."

Silent, the smile gone, Paul looked down and fidgeted with backpack, tightening and then loosening the straps. "That's my business," he said finally. There was no anger or disrespect in his tone, just blunt finality. The issue was out of bounds. And for Jason the matter was no longer a lingering curiosity; something seemed very wrong. But despite his best efforts, he could think of no way to bring the matter up again, so they drove the dark streets in silence. Jason turned the car onto Hollow Stone Drive and they rolled quietly past the new park, its deserted playgrounds and picnic areas pale blue in the moonlight. At the curb in front of the Coldwell house Jason stopped the car.

"Thanks for the ride," said Paul.

The dome light came on when he opened his door and got out.

"One last thing," said Jason quickly.

Reluctantly, Paul looked back into the car. Jason, his face half-shadowed in the dim yellow light, seemed to struggle for words. When at last he spoke, his eyes dropped and his voice seemed tentative, unsure. "I'm not trying to, you know, mess with your business or anything, but I just wanted to say if you ever need something, you can give me a call. It's no big thing. I got tons of time on my hands this summer and I get a check from the Marines every month and . . ."

Jason saw the expression change on Paul's face, the sudden recognition in his eyes. It was the money. He shouldn't have said anything about the money. He trailed off and searched for someway to backtrack.

"Did Lou tell you I needed cash?" asked Paul.

"No, he just said something about a motel and raised rent and I saw your truck up for sale and figured that you might need—"

"Listen, Jason," Paul interrupted, speaking now as though he were thoroughly fatigued. "Whatever Lou said to you shouldn't have been said." He got out of the car and shut the door, squatted down and looked through the open window. "I appreciate the gesture, but there's nothing you can do for us. Do me a favor and just forget the whole thing."

They looked at one another in silence. Then Paul slung his backpack up onto his shoulders and without looking back walked away. Jason looked after him until the door had shut; then he shifted the car into drive and turned across the street and into the carport of his own house.

■　■　■

Paul dropped heavily onto the floor against the living room wall and sat with his head in his hands. So his neighbor now knew, or at least suspected. And so, apparently, did his son. He'd tried so hard to keep his sickness from Lou, to protect him from the blunt weight of the truth, but as with so many other things in his life, he'd failed to achieve his goal. As the weight of the realization began to press down on him, he wondered when Lou had first seen through his lies.

After a few minutes he got up and in a box beside the stone fireplace found his old photo album. He sat down again, set the album on his lap, and opened to a random page near the end. He looked down at a photograph of himself, about fifteen years old, smiling in front of a man and woman, who each rested a hand on one of his shoulders. Built from strong square lines, the man wore a red sweater with white snowflakes woven through the torso. Beside him stood the woman, her black hair like silk on her shoulders, her eyes blinked shut. The stone fireplace stood in the background; the picture had been taken in this same room. The caption:

Paul, Mom, and Dad
Esperanza, Thanksgiving, 1984

Paul leaned back against the wall. He'd thought that perhaps the memories might comfort him, but they only sharpened the pain. He tried to slam the album shut, but it dropped down to the carpet between his knees and fell open to the final page, where a fading polaroid had been taped crookedly beneath the clear plastic cover. Although it had been taken about the same time as the last picture, Paul looked very different. His face was thinner, almost gaunt, and his dark eyes were focused on the floor in front of him. In the background, his arm around a thin smiling blonde, stood a tall man with a narrow serious face, flat black hair, and deep-set eyes. It was Melvin. The caption, written by different hand than the last one, read:

My Birthday, Feb. 1985

Paul, unblinking and still, stared at his uncle as though entranced. Seeing Melvin's face, remembering the events the had taken him to Kanab, thinking about his own sickness now, he felt that same buzzing rage he'd felt on his first day at the mine. It was too much. He grabbed the binder by the back cover and flung it across the room. It flew apart in the air, pages and photographs tearing free and scattered down to the bare carpetless floor. The album itself crashed against the wall.

Paul looked at the loose photographs and pages, at the binder half-open on the carpetless floor. One of the photographs lay near his foot. He picked it up and looked at it, grimaced, and flicked it away. For a while he merely stared at the mess. Then, as though very tired, he slouched back against the wall and closed his eyes.

■ ■ ■

The crash startled Lou. He lay awake on his mattress, trying to slow his breathing. Although he'd left his hiding place in the trees by the irrigation ditch after the first round, when his father's victory seemed certain, and run home as fast as he could manage, he still only beat Paul through the door by a minute or two. He listened now for some other sound, but all was quiet again.

Eventually his father's footsteps moved down the hall. The hinges of the bedroom door creaked and he knew Paul was looking in on him. For what seemed a very long time, there was no sound at all, and Lou wondered if perhaps Paul had slipped away and left the door open. But then the hinges creaked again and the latch clicked shut and a moment later he heard Paul go into the bathroom and start the shower.

CHAPTER 14

*T*he morning sun angled through the kitchen window and lit the dust, thousands of tiny specks like snow from a domed Christmas scene. The yellow rotary phone mounted on the wall was ringing, a tinny sound that wavered as though about to quit. It rang and rang and rang—whoever was on the other end was, if nothing else, persistent—before Lou stumbled into the kitchen with sleep in his eyes to answer it.

"Hello."

"Give me Paul Coldwell."

"He works mornings."

"Not this one, he's not."

"What?"

"This is Boyd Grummet, Paul's boss. You know where he is?"

"He's not there?"

"I take it he's not home."

"Hold on."

Lou put the phone on the counter and hurried from the kitchen. The master bedroom was empty except for two boxes, set side-by-side, piled with clothes, and Paul's mattress, on which, hidden by a bright Mexican-style blanket, lay Paul. Lou gently shook his father awake. He rolled over and slowly opened his bloodshot eyes. His cheek was creased where he'd slept on it.

"Someone's on the phone for you," Lou said.

"Who?" asked Paul, his throat full of sand.

"Some guy from your work."

It was then that Paul noticed the sunlight in the window. His eyes widened. He looked at his wrist, but he wasn't wearing a watch. "What time is it?" he asked, throwing back the blanket and jumping to his feet.

Lou shrugged. "That guy's still waitin on the phone."

Paul hurried out of the room. Lou heard him pick up the phone. "This is Paul."

Lou walked back down the hall, intending to go back into the kitchen, but this time as he passed the living room he noticed the mess, the photos and album pages strewn across the bare floor, the album itself torn at the spine. As he knelt and looked at one of the pictures, he could hear his father in the kitchen repeating the same two words every few seconds, "Yes, sir." Then, after a longer pause, he said, "I understand the seriousness, sir. I just forgot to set my alarm. I'll be in your office in a few minutes." The ringer clanked as Paul slammed the phone down.

Paul hurried back toward his room, but stopped in the hall when he saw Lou kneeling on the floor in the living room. He had the broken album in one hand and was gathering up the photos one by one with the other. Lou paused and looked back over his shoulder. "What happened here?" he asked.

But there was no easy explanation, and no time for a long one. "I . . . I just . . . Last night . . . " Paul sighed deeply and gave up. "We'll talk when I get home," he said, and then he hurried down the hall to get dressed.

Lou turned back to the photos and continued gathering them up.

■ ■ ■

Jason's conversation with Paul the previous night ran through his mind all morning; the intuition that he was supposed to help them, that this was why he'd been saved, wouldn't leave him. At last he hit a few medical websites and searched for possible causes of chronic headaches. The results ranged from migraines to stress to strained eyes to stress to brain tumors. When he read that secondary symptoms for tumors can include, among other things, unexplained nausea and vomiting, he felt the darkness, the doubt clouding his mind once more.

By the early afternoon, as a sheet of gray watercolor clouds pushed over the western mountains, Jason made up his mind. He had to talk to Lou, but he had to raise the matter gently, since he didn't know how much the boy knew and how much he only suspected. His knee brace strapped on, he set off as quickly as he could manage to Prospector Street and the trail up to Fire Creek. He met Lou only a few hundred yards past the chain-link fence; the boy came fast around a bend and they nearly collided.

"Jason!" said Lou, startled. "You got to whistle or something. I about lost my breakfast."

"Sorry. I didn't think you'd be coming back so early."

"Looked like it was going to rain. What're you doin?"

"Thought I come pay you a visit, see how things were going."

"Almost finished," said Lou. "Few more days and I'll have it."

"You think your dad'll like it?"

"Hope so."

"How is your dad?" Jason asked.

"Great," said Lou, but Jason thought the answer sounded a bit hollow.

They walked for a time through the trees and spoke of inconsequential things, and although Jason constantly looked for some opening, some way of turning the conversation back to Paul without seeming too obvious, the right moment never arose. Eventually they came to the fence, which Jason climbed over and Lou squirmed under. When they neared their homes on Hollow Stone Drive, it began to rain. The heavy drops tapped loudly on the plastic roof of the carport and spotted the hot blacktop before evaporating almost as quickly as they appeared. They stopped in the street and stood looking at the Coldwell house. Jason was about to speak, when Lou, his face troubled, turned to him and spoke first.

"I need your help," he said. No context, no introduction. He just said it.

"What's wrong?"

"My dad."

Jason's stomach dropped and he hoped his fears were not about to be confirmed.

"I think something's wrong with him," Lou continued, his voice strained. It was raining harder now and a few drops had spotted his glasses. "I didn't want to tell anyone, but I don't know what to do. You're the only one I really know here, and . . . I thought . . . well, I been prayin for him but . . . And last night he wrecked the photo album his mom made for him. He's always taken care of that album . . ." Lou took his glasses off and wiped them on his shirt. He looked like he was going to cry. "I don't know what to do," he said.

Jason put his hands on Lou's shoulders and spoke with deliberate calm, as though he could influence Lou's mood with his tone. "I want to help you, Lou, but I need you to tell me everything you know about what's been happening."

Lou began to speak, his voice quivering. He explained that right before they'd moved to Melvin's place Paul had grown very sad and quiet. Before that he started complaining about headaches and went to see a few doctors. Sometimes, during those first weeks, Lou would wake to hear his father weeping in the early morning hours.

Melvin, Lou explained, seemed also to know something was wrong, and after they moved into his motel he kept asking Paul if he'd made his final arrangements. Lou said that one day Paul just snapped. He went outside and stood in front of the motel and looked at their room and wouldn't say anything for almost an hour. Then he left Lou with Melvin for a day and drove off "to take care of some business in Arizona," as he put it. The week after he got back, he'd contacted Esperanza Copper, quit his job at the auto shop, and explained that they'd be moving back to his parents' old house, where they wouldn't have to pay rent.

"That's when we came here," said Lou. "I think he's really sick."

It was raining hard now, and their shoulders and hair were soaked. Lou was scared; Jason could see that clearly, but he still couldn't see how to help.

"What can I do?" he asked at last.

Lou said it was pointless to talk to Paul directly; he'd tried that countless times now. He said the only thing he could think of would be to talk to Melvin. He's the only one who knew what was going on. At Jason's request Lou gave him Melvin's last name—Littlefoot—and told him that his motel in Kanab was simply called Melvin's Motel. But as soon as he'd given out the information, he immediately seemed to regret it.

"I shouldn't have told you this," he said, wiping his sleeve across his nose. "Please don't tell my dad I told you." And then, without another word, he spun away and set off across the street at a pace somewhere between walking and jogging. Still crouched at the roadside, Jason called to him, but he didn't turn back. When the Coldwells' door clapped shut, Jason's head fell forward and his eyes closed. It was quiet then. Just the patter of the rain and the occasional rush of the wind.

CHAPTER 15

"For what city, please?" asked the recording.

"Kanab, Utah," Jason said. He sat at the kitchen table, the cordless pressed to his ear, a notepad and pen in hand.

"And for what listing?"

"Melvin Littlefoot."

"One moment, please."

The phone line clicked twice, and then an operator's voice spoke: "I'm sorry, sir, but that number is unlisted."

"Unlisted?"

"Yes, sir."

"But you still have the number, right?"

"I'm sorry, sir, but I can't give out that information."

"But this is an emergency."

"Sir, if it's an emergency, please hang up and dial 911."

Jason grimaced, tried to regroup. He kicked his chair back and paced across the kitchen.

"What if I was family—could you give it to me then?"

"If you was family, you probably wouldn't be calling me."

"I really need that number."

"I'm sorry, sir."

"It's just sitting there on your screen, isn't it? You're looking at it right now."

"Is there anything else I can do for you, sir?"

"Melvin would want you to give me his number. I'm an old friend. He'd thank you for it."

"Goodbye, sir."

"No, wait—"

The phone clicked, the operator was gone. He called back, this time asked for Melvin's Motel. The number he got turned out to be disconnected. He slammed the phone down on the base and sat at the kitchen table. Then, after a moment's thought, he stood again and dialed another number.

"No one is available to take your—"

"Rooster," Jason cut in. "It's me."

"Jason! What's going on, bro?"

"You still got that old Chevy?"

"Yeah."

"Good. Tell me you don't have any plans for the next day or two."

"Okay. I don't have any plans. Why?"

"Road trip. I could really use some company."

"Where to?"

"Kanab."

The line went quiet for a moment.

"All right," Rooster said, as if it were all perfectly normal.

"All right?"

"Sure. I got nothing to do. Why not go to Kanab? When do we leave?"

"The sooner the better."

■ ■ ■

"You drive," said Rooster, tossing the keys to Jason. Rooster was the proud owner of a brown 1979 Chevrolet Impala, a car at least twice as long as any you'd find on the road today and at least three times as heavy. Rooster joked that cars like this had kept US steel mills open through the seventies.

It was a fine Thursday afternoon—high gauzy clouds, hot sun, no wind to speak of. They filled up with gas in Esperanza and then set out on U.S. 89, following it south toward Kanab.

"I never asked you about the tournament," Rooster said, making conversation. "How'd it go?"

"As well as expected."

"Coldwell win?"

"Yeah. He fights this tough Hawaiian dude, Kawika, in the next round. How'd things go with Lou?"

"Interesting night."

"What's that mean?"

Rooster told Jason about the sparkler, the bucket of fireworks, the thirty seconds of chaos.

"How come things like that always happen to you, Rooster?" asked Jason, laughing.

"Good karma, I guess."

"What'd Lou say about it?"

"I don't know. He took off right after. Never got a chance to ask him."

"He left?"

"I went to grab a broom and when I came back he was AWOL."

"What time did he leave?"

"Ten, maybe. Ten-fifteen at the latest."

"Paul's fight didn't start until eleven." Jason thought for a moment, tried to remember the details of his conversation with Lou the day after the fights. "You know, he didn't ask me any questions about his dad's fight."

"Maybe his pop filled him in."

"I don't know."

"What's done is done," said Rooster, shrugging. He unzipped his backpack and produced a rainbow of snack cakes, candies, cookies, and crackers. It was as though he'd knocked over a candy store and made off with a sample from every shelf. "You want some snacks, dude?" he asked, taking a jumbo bag of black licorice out for himself.

"No, thanks," Jason said. He was still thinking about the tournament, wondering where Lou might've hidden.

"You sure? I got everything. Little Debbies, gummi worms, candy corns. You name it. I even got some Reese's Pieces."

"I'm good."

"You ever wonder how Reese's Pieces got picked up for *E.T.*?"

"Never thought about it."

"I was thinking the other day that Spielberg probably bought himself a lion's share of Reese's stock right before filming and figured it'd be a quick way to make a few thousand smackers."

"Didn't *E.T.* gross like twelve quadrillion dollars?"

"Four-hundred thirty-five million domestic."

"That is a freakish thing to know, Rooster. Anyway, my point is this—all that money and he'd still go through the effort for a few thousand?"

"Those rich dudes aren't like you and me. Their gears are always churning out new ways to raise their net worth." Rooster bit off the end of a licorice. Chewing, he added, "Money's like Chinese food, bro. Feels good for about thirty minutes and then you get hungry again."

"I bet you know all about that," Jason teased, patting Rooster's gut.

"I got a gland problem, dude. This fat retention's genetic."

Rooster finished his licorice and tore into a Twinkie. Genetics indeed, thought Jason, shaking his head. But he was glad for the ride and the company so he said nothing more about it. Fifteen minutes later, however, Rooster was asleep, goodies spread across his lap, his backpack open on the floor between his feet.

■ ■ ■

They arrived in Kanab an hour after sundown and checked into one of the discount franchise motels. Jason thought of staying in Melvin's Motel, but decided he was too tired and would wait until the morning to talk to the man. Their room was small, old, but clean. Rooster spread a thin blanket over the floor and lay down, claiming it was good for the lower back. "The best of the old samurai slept on hardwood every night," he said.

"That's because their masters took the beds," said Jason. He flopped out on the mattress and closed his eyes. Not thirty seconds later a sound like a 747 taking off. Rooster, snoring. Jason groaned and pulled a pillow over his head. With Rooster on the floor there was little chance he'd roll over. It was going to be a long night.

■ ■ ■

The sun was unbearable, and now by some fluke Austen had sprained his ankle. To make matters worse, Rodney was missing—at least Jason hadn't seen him, yet none of the others said anything about it or seemed concerned.

They sat down in the shade beneath the wall to wait for Austen's ride, and for a time a woman in a burka stood at the corner watching them, her dark eyes wide and beautiful between the slits of her veil. Somehow, Jason felt he knew her, but this made no sense at all. He almost called to her, but she turned suddenly and disappeared around a corner. Where was Rodney? Jason wondered, looking after her. Rodney would've known what was going on.

And then suddenly there he was, far off on a parallel street, visible only for a second as he passed between two buildings. He was walking with his wife and daughters, the four of them holding hands.

Jason stood. Rodney!

But he was gone.

Suddenly the sand was everywhere, spinning in from the desert, eddying around corners and through broken windows, forcing Jason to shield his eyes. Then, just as suddenly as it had come, it was gone.

Cautiously, Jason opened his eyes. There, across the street stood a man of Asian descent with a face that in some ways mirrored Jason's. Jason knew him once.

Dad?

The man smiled.

Dad!

A single gunshot rang out, startling Jason. Instinctively he dropped for cover. Now someone was screaming about a sniper, and Davison was screaming for everyone to get down. Others were shooting of rounds in quick bursts. Jason looked up, but the man was gone.

Then the wall exploded and all went dark.

■ ■ ■

When Jason woke, Rooster, already dressed, was standing at the window, peeking out through the curtains. "Just keeping an eye on the car," he said, when he saw Jason.

"Anything of interest?"

"Squad car came through about an hour ago."

"Keep me posted."

Jason showered and dressed and then he and Rooster checked out. They stopped at a fast food joint for some breakfast, where Jason looked up Melvin's Motel in the phone directory. The address put it way out on the east side of town.

Twenty minutes later they arrived. The motel was just what Jason had imagined: single story, cracked pink stucco, green doors, stubby trees, oil-stained parking lot. Across the street, a barbershop, a laundromat, and a sleazy loan office. Rooster waited in the car and worked on a bag of pretzels while Jason went to the office.

The door buzzed when he entered. The office was small, painted lipstick red. A fan whirred from a mount in the corner, fluttering the pages of a few outdated tourist brochures. A man with a bad combover and a shirt that had somehow made it unscathed out of the disco seventies walked from the back room. "What can I do you for?" he asked.

"I'm looking for Melvin Littlefoot."

"He's the owner."

"Is he here?"

"Nope."

"You know when he'll be here?"

"Nope."

"You have any idea where I can find him?"

"Nope."

Jason stood there at the counter, staring at the man's combover, thinking that there must be something more he could say. Outside the office window, a red pickup turned into the handicap place and an old man with long hair pulled back under a wide-brimmed hat stepped out. He wore dark lizard boots, which clicked against the tile floor of the office when he entered. The bald man quit leaning on the counter and stood at rigid attention.

"You checkin in or out?" the old man asked, without really looking at Jason.

"Neither. I was looking for someone."

"He was looking for you, Mel," said the clerk.

Melvin turned to Jason as though seeing him for the first time. His face was deeply creased and his irises were the color of charcoal.

"I know you?" he asked.

"No," said Jason. He felt intimidated and he didn't like it. To compensate, he spoke more boldly than perhaps he should have. "I'm here about your nephew, Paul Coldwell."

One corner of Melvin's mouth turned down, almost as though he were chewing a shoot of wheat. He looked hard at Jason. "If this is about money, you come to the wrong buckaroo," he said, his voice low, gravelly.

"It's not about money."

Melvin swore under his breath. He turned to the clerk. "How many units filled last night?"

"Three," said the clerk.

Melvin swore again.

"There's a guy comin out to clean the stains in twenty-two," he said. "Go out and meet him."

"Yessir," said the clerk, and he hurried out to the parking lot.

"Come back and sit down," said Melvin, already halfway through the door into the backroom. Jason followed him back and took a seat on an old corduroy sofa across from the desk. For a half-minute Melvin sorted through the papers stacked on the desktop until finally, without looking up, he said, "You just goin to sit there?"

Jason leaned forward in his chair. "Like I was sayin, I came about Paul."

Melvin was still sorting through papers, pausing now and again to read a paragraph or two. Jason cleared his voice, spoke louder. "I think something may be wrong with him."

"Of course there's something wrong with him."

Jason hesitated. "Would you mind telling me what you know about it?"

"Sure. He's a jackass—that's what's wrong with him." Melvin looked up. "Who'd you say you were again?"

"Jason Chang. I'm Paul's neighbor." He added after a moment's thought, "A friend of the family."

"You drove all the way from Esperanza?"

"I needed some answers, mostly for Lou's sake."

"Lou," said Melvin as though the name filled his mouth with lemon juice. "I was wonderin when we'd get to him."

Melvin reclined his chair and looked at Jason with that same stone-hard expression. "I ain't takin that boy. You got to understand that first and foremost."

"What?"

"I did my good deed already. I don't need another Coldwell boy to raise."

"Why would you take Lou in?"

A smile broke across Melvin's face, an unpleasant smile full of irony. "He didn't tell you."

"Tell me what?"

"The head," said Melvin, rapping a knuckle on the side of his own skull. "The tumor."

Jason felt as though the energy had suddenly been drained from his body. The news was not unexpected, but it still hit him hard. Melvin, seeing the abrupt change in Jason's face, sighed and turned his attention back to his papers. "Listen, Chong—or whatever your name was—clearly you have no clue what's goin on here, so maybe you should get back home, ask Paul these questions, and quit wastin my time."

Jason stared at Melvin. He didn't know what to do, only knew what he wanted to do—reach across the desk, grab the old man by the collar, and shake him until his teeth rattled. Incredible that Paul could live with such a man. "I'm not leaving until you tell me what else you know," Jason said at last.

Melvin made a few notes on one of the papers. "Is that a threat, Mr. Chong?"

"It is what it is." Jason leaned forward, put both hands on the desk. "I drove all the way down here just to speak with you. Least you could do is give me five minutes."

Melvin sighed again. He reclined back, took off his hat, and put it down on the desk. "Five minutes," he said, looking at his watch.

Jason asked the questions as quickly as he could, and as the seconds ticked by, Melvin told him in a voice full of sarcasm and condescension about Paul's tumor. A time bomb, he said. Could sit for a year, could sit for a month, but sooner or later it's goin off. Paul's doctor, he explained, had no hope: the tumor was inoperable. All they could do was treat symptoms. Shortly after Paul had been diagnosed in late February he'd begged Melvin to let him move back into the motel. He talked some nonsense about wanting to save money.

But Melvin figured Paul had an angle, that he was trying to arrange it so that after he died Melvin would have to take Lou in. And Melvin wanted none of that. He'd already done it once. Despite never marrying, he'd taken Paul in out of respect for his dead sister, Paul's mother, after she and her husband had been killed in some freak explosion at an Esperanza Copper warehouse.

"When was that?" Jason interrupted, his face suddenly drawn.

"What difference does it make?"

"Just answer the question. Was it in eighty-four?"

Melvin counted the numbers in his head. "Yeah," he said at last. "December of '84. How'd you know that?"

Jason said he'd heard about it from his mother and told Melvin to continue. For a time, although he heard Melvin speaking, his mind made no sense of the words. Instead, several thoughts and emotions flashed across his mind almost simultaneously: he wondered why his mother hadn't told him, he wondered why both of the Coldwells were in the warehouse with his own father that day, and he felt a sudden bond with Paul, a feeling that one minute earlier, he'd not had.

By the time he remembered that Melvin was speaking, the old man had moved on to Paul's performance in school. Paul had blown it, Melvin was saying. Flunked all his classes after his parents died and dropped out of school. He didn't make any friends. He didn't work. A few of the neighbors thought he was depressed, but Melvin knew better. He knew Paul just wanted attention. He knew Paul was lazy. So he sent him to a military-style boarding school, paid the tuition out of his own pocket. But Paul was thrown out for fighting. After that he started boxing. Won a few fights and impressed a few trainers, who put him on the regional circuit. Then he met a girl from Arizona, she got pregnant, they got married, and Paul had to quit boxing and take a real job.

"After that he was out of my life," said Melvin. "Which was fine by me. Didn't see or hear from him until he shows up at my door a few months ago, begging me to give him a free room. He told me about the tumor, and that's when I knew what he was up to with Lou."

"So why'd he leave?" asked Jason.

"I started chargin him for the room."

"Why would you do that to him?"

"I told you, I already raised one Coldwell boy." Melvin glanced at his watch. "Three, two, one, time. Have a safe trip home, Mr. Chong."

Jason stood and looked down at Melvin, watched him sort through his papers. "If you're not taking the boy in, who is?" he asked.

"Time's up, Chong."

"Who's taking the boy?" asked Jason, louder.

Melvin kicked back his chair and stood and looked hard at Jason. "Not my problem," he barked.

The two men stood in the small office, separated only by the desk, their eyes locked. Jason wasn't backing down. The old man could see that. At last he spun round, opened the file drawer, searched, pulled out an index card and flicked it toward Jason. It hit him in the leg and fell to the floor. Jason picked it up. It was an old Rolodex card, written up for someone named Teresa Roberts in Flagstaff, Arizona.

"What's this?" asked Jason.

"It's for the person you should be talkin to." Melvin sat again, took up his papers. "Paul's ex, Lou's mom."

Jason put the card in his pocket and walked out of the office.

■ ■ ■

Rooster was asleep again, reclined back in the passenger seat. Jason got in and started the car. Rooster opened his eyes. "How'd it go?"

"I got what I needed."

"You don't look too happy about it."

"It was an . . . interesting conversation. You got any more time to waste, Rooster?"

"Sure. Why?"

"We're goin to Flagstaff."

"Never been there before."

"It's your lucky day."

They got back on U.S. 89 and followed it south through the desert into Arizona, where dark hawks turned slow circles against a white sky and heat waves shimmered on the highway. In the late morning hours they climbed through the lodgepole pine forests into Flagstaff. They ate tacos for lunch, then hunted down the address, at last found it in an apartment complex in a poor neighborhood. Rooster parked the car in the shade of an elm, took out his candy bag, and said he'd wait in the car again.

The buildings were old, gray brick, mostly dead lawns, cracked sidewalks. The swimming pool was only half-full and two children's floaty toys bobbed in the middle. A heavy woman in black sweat-pants sat on her doorstep, watching him.

"You know where 7F is?" asked Jason.

The woman raised a hand, gestured vaguely to the far end of the complex. Jason followed one of the walks in the direction she'd pointed and found the number, a bottom-floor apartment. The door-mat and cement around it were littered with cigarette butts. He rang the bell.

The dead bolt jiggled and the door opened an inch or two, just enough for the chain still locked inside to snap tight. A woman peeked out. Though Jason couldn't see her completely, he could tell that she was short, thin, with long hair bleached unnaturally blonde and a sun-toughened face. She looked thirty-five, maybe forty years old.

"I'm looking for Teresa Roberts. I was told she lives here."

"What you want with her?"

Jason cleared his throat. "It's about her son, Lou."

The woman unlatched the chain on the door and opened it fully. She wore denim cutoffs that reached midway down her bony thighs and a tanktop that didn't do much to cover the black straps of her bra. No shoes. A beaded chain around the ankle and silver rings on two of her toes. "I'm Teresa Roberts," she said. "Who are you?"

"Someone who's trying to help," said Jason.

"Is Paul dead?"

"No. I'm just, um . . . I'm just checking on things for him."

"What's there to check on? He calls me every week from his job to make sure I'm stickin to his plan."

"His plan?"

Teresa's lips tightened into a frown. She exhaled slowly, as though releasing steam. "Paul sent you to spy on me, didn't he?" Her eyes closed, she ran her hands back through her bleached hair as though she wanted to pull it out. "I can't handle this right now," she hissed through gritted teeth.

"I'm not here to spy on you, Ms. Roberts," said Jason. He had no idea where any of this was going, nor what had gotten it started.

"Then what are you here for? Is it about the money?"

"Yes," said Jason, grasping at anything that might move them for-ward. "It's about the money."

"I knew it. I knew he'd do this to me. And after I tried to change my entire life for him!" Again Teresa pulled at her hair. "I can't handle this right now," she repeated, as though it were her mantra. "I can't handle it!"

"Paul has the money," said Jason, trying to calm her.

Teresa's pale eyes stopped skittering around and focused on him. The stress had washed from her face like rain. "All twenty thousand?" she asked.

Teresa must've seen the change in Jason's face, the sudden recognition of what she was really asking for, because her eyes widened and she grabbed Jason's arm and began speaking quickly, rambling, throwing sentences together almost incoherently: "I'm not a bad person. This was all Paul's idea. He's the one that showed up all of a sudden tellin me he's dyin and needin me to take the kid back. He's the one that made me sign up for AA and got me a part-timer. He knows I don't have no cash. I couldn't take the kid without help. I really am tryin to make this work, but after all, he's the one that wanted full custody after I left him . . . Hey! Where you goin?"

Jason had started walking away. He wanted nothing more than to be away from this woman, to leave her run-down apartment and her broken life and her frigid rationalizations. The thought of Paul handing over twenty-thousand so that she could support Lou was unbearable.

"I'm not a bad person," Teresa called after him.

He kept walking, didn't look back.

"I'm not a bad person!" she screamed.

Jason turned the corner away from the building.

CHAPTER 16

*J*ason sat in the passenger seat, looking out at the lodgepole pines, watching them slide past the old Chevy. There was nothing he could do. Paul would die. Lou would be sent to live with Teresa Roberts. Or if the money wasn't there, maybe he'd end up with the state. Maybe that way would be best. Either way, though, there was nothing he could do—no point to any of this.

Rooster, sensing the change in Jason, respected the silence. It wasn't until they were back in Utah that either of them spoke.

"You believe in God, Rooster?" Jason asked, still looking out the passenger window.

"Yeah."

"You believe God is good?"

"Yeah."

"And he's okay with all these people suffering and dying before their time?"

"He had to have some way for us to check out, bro. We weren't meant to stay here forever."

Jason let his head fall back against the headrest and he closed his eyes. "Still," he said, "there must be a better way."

"You know, Jason," said Rooster, "the Persians used to have this curse, the worst you could put on a man. Went something like this— may your every wish be granted the moment you wish it."

"Sounds really bad."

"I'm serious, man. Think about it. Everything you ever want or could want, yours, without any effort at all. Nothing to work for. Nothing to hope for. Nothing to achieve. Nothing to do at all. That's hell if anything is."

Jason opened his eyes, watched the cars moving over the road ahead.

"Is that how life really should be, bro?" Rooster continued, after a while. "I mean, pull back and think about what you're saying for a minute. No pain. No suffering. If so, where do you draw the line? Discomfort? Annoyance?" Rooster paused, let the questions hang in the air for a moment.

"When I was a kid I suffered," he continued. "I was different, weird. I came from a weird family. I remember this one day I was lying on the tire swing and these big sixth graders pinned me down and stole my clothes. They tied my arms around the tire and left me there in my superman underwear . . . No one even noticed I was gone until after school when the custodian found me." Rooster paused, laughed at the absurdity of it all. "Man, there were times when I seriously considered killing myself. But now I'm a stronger man for it. I know who I am and I don't apologize for it. Would you take that away from me because it was painful?"

"I never knew that about you, Rooster," Jason said quietly. He looked over at his friend with newfound respect. "But the thing is, that story ended well. Other stories don't. A few months ago my best friend's story ended in Afghanistan when a sniper's bullet dropped him. He left behind a wife and two kids. And now someone I know is dying of a brain tumor. His kid loves him, prays for him every night, but he's going to die anyway. Any five-year-old kid could tell you that's not the way the story's supposed to go."

Rooster sighed and for a time seemed to be thinking. "We're all going to end up as fertilizer, bro—it's only a matter of time. And if R.I.P. were the last letters on everyone's final pages, then I guess those lives you mentioned would be sad and hopeless. But I don't think that is the end of their stories. I think they've just finished up a few of the key middle chapters, that's all. The best parts—happy reunions when your friend sees his wife and kids again and Lou sees his father again—they're all yet to come. Pain always looks different with perspective. And any five-year-old could tell you a story without conflict and struggle in the middle isn't a story worth telling or hearing."

Jason looked out the window. For a time they drove in silence. Then Jason realized what Rooster had said.

"Did you say when *Lou* sees his father again?"

Rooster offered a sad smile. "You don't really think I'm that dense, do you?"

Jason sat back in his chair and watched the highway ahead shimmering in the summer sun. "So what do we do, man? What do we do to help them?"

"Pray," said Rooster. "And if this is the end of Paul's chapter here, we do whatever we can to make it as good as it can be."

Jason wanted to believe what Rooster was saying; he wanted to believe in the ultimate goodness of God and his ways. But looking at the story from this end, it was still hard for him to believe it was worth it.

CHAPTER 17

*T*he warm colors of dusk shone on the clouds scattered across the sky, and to the east the peaks above Fire Creek had darkened to shades of violet. Standing outside the old carport, holding up his ten-speed, Paul Coldwell looked at the sky, at the high peaks, at the flock of starlings that darted low over the rooftop and round the high trees in back of the house. He wore the same cotton shorts and black hooded sweatshirt, and the old backpack was slung over his shoulders. Lou sat on the porch steps.

"Nights like this my dad and me used to drive up to Fire Creek and watch the dark come."

"Sounds like a good time," said Lou.

"I wish you could've seen it like it was back then. But I guess everything fades eventually."

He pushed his ten-speed down the broken driveway.

"Good luck tonight, Dad," said Lou.

"Thanks," said Paul. "Don't wait up for me."

Then, as the blunt harmonies of the mine train's whistle echoed across the valley, he got onto his bike and pedaled away.

When he had gone, Lou went into the house, put on his shoes and a black sweatshirt, and slipped out the back door.

■ ■ ■

As the old Chevy Impala moved down the switchbacks into Esperanza, a full moon, silver against the dark angles of the mountains, rose into the sky. Rooster sat behind the wheel, Jason in the passenger seat with the window down, the cool clean wind in his face. Across the valley, perhaps four miles distant, he saw the floodlights over Big Sammy's restaurant, mere pinpricks of light against the vacant field beyond. The fights. He'd forgotten it was Friday.

"What time is it, Rooster?"

"About ten."

"Can you drop me off at Fat Sammy's?"

"Don't tell me you want to watch that nonsense."

"Paul's fighting Kawika tonight."

"Fat Sammy's it is."

■ ■ ■

Lou slipped through the darkness beneath the gnarled trees. He walked slowly, always in the deepest shadows near the irrigation ditch, until the noise of the crowd surrounded him and the glow from the spotlights over the boxing ring shone through the breaks in the leaves. There, in the deep shadows, where he had a long view past the bleachers to the ring, he settled down to wait.

■ ■ ■

Beside the ring, his shirt stripped off, his helmet strapped on, Paul stood swinging his arms and jumping lightly, as though skipping rope. Across from him on a folding chair, a small man with a lit cigarette pressed between his lips worked at lacing up Kawika's black gloves. Kawika sat with his eyes closed, his face calm and confident. Behind him, at the edge of the light, Jason Chang walked around the corner of the restaurant and took a place against the back wall, away from the other men. Paul saw him and turned quickly away.

A minute later Sammy climbed into the ring and waved his hairy arms for attention. When the crowd had quieted, he began his announcement: "In case you been in jail or something, tonight's the second round. Four fights tonight. Semifinals are next Friday, and the final match is on Sunday afternoon. Also, you all keep it in your thick skulls that we'll be here next year to do this all over again, so first thing tomorrow get out the punch bags and start trainin away those beer bellies."

He paused and consulted his index card. "First up we got Kawika Makanoa and Paul Coldwell. We'll start as soon as both fighters are set."

Paul lowered his head, breathed in and out deeply a few times, and climbed through the ropes.

"You both ready?" the same fat referee asked, looking at both fighters in turn. When both nodded, he signaled to the ringside table, where the timekeeper, seated next to Sammy, triggered his stopwatch and blasted the air horn. As a few spectators shouted violent encouragements, Paul and Kawika stepped out of their corners. Paul moved with his left foot leading, his left shoulder angled toward Kawika, both gloves held steady about ten inches in front of his face. Though Paul was well-muscled, sharing the ring with Kawika he looked somewhat thin and short. As they side-stepped, changing their positions by calculated angles, Paul shot off two speculative jabs. Kawika stepped back and lowered his gloves to stomach level, almost daring Paul to fire a hook at his face. Instead, Paul jabbed again and side-stepped quickly to avoid a circling right from Kawika.

When the air horn signaled the end of the first round, neither fighter had managed to do any damage to the other. Paul had kept Kawika back with annoying jabs, while Kawika had launched tremendous hooks that, while capable of knocking down small houses, took too long in developing and were easily avoided with good footwork. Sweat dripping down his face and into his eyes, Paul returned to his corner, where a stool had been set for him. Across the ring, the small man who'd helped Kawika earlier to lace his gloves now squirted water into Kawika's mouth and said something to him and pointed across the ring at Paul and laughed. Kawika smiled.

Paul looked down from the ring at Carlos Alvarez, who was sitting at the folding table next to Sammy and the timekeeper.

"Hey, Carlos," Paul said, his voice slurred by his mouthpiece, "how bout some water?"

Carlos took a water bottle from the table and climbed up to Paul's corner. He fished Paul's mouthpiece out with his gloved finger and helped him take a drink; then he dumped the rest of the water over Paul's sweating face.

"Ten seconds," the timekeeper shouted.

Carlos returned Paul's mouthpiece and took the stool and climbed back down from the ring. The air horn blasted again and Paul and Kawika angled out of their corners to meet one another.

The first two minutes of the second round passed like the first—Paul nimble on his feet, shooting out cautious jabs to keep Kawika away; Kawika swinging heavy impatient punches that missed badly. Near the end of the round, as he launched two quick lefts, Paul planted his back foot on a paper cup someone had thrown into the ring. His foot slipped and he dropped his guard instinctively, if only for a second, to catch his balance. In that moment, whether by luck or by skill, Kawika stepped forward and brought a right from his hip into Paul's ribs, dropping him heavily to his knees. When the air horn sounded a few seconds later, ending the round, Paul was still doubled over, his arms folded across his mid-section, wheezing and wincing in pain. The referee, who'd made it to six, stopped counting, waved his hands over his head, and, clearly disappointed, shouted for all to hear, "Coldwell saved by the bell! No knock-out!"

"You all right, man?" Carlos Alvarez said, stooping close to Paul's face so as to be heard over the shouting from the bleachers.

"Fine," Paul wheezed. Still wincing, he raised up and looked at the doctor.

"You got to stand up," Carlos said, reaching around Paul's back with one arm to help him to his feet. Somebody passed up a stool and Paul sat down.

"Move your arms," Carlos ordered, pushing Paul's gloves away from his mid-section. As he pressed his palm against the ribs, Paul grunted.

"Might be broken," Carlos said.

"Not broken," Paul managed, still struggling to catch his breath.

"How would you know?"

"Broke em before. Felt different."

Carlos looked closely at Paul; then he shrugged and climbed out of the ring, leaving Paul alone in his corner.

As the next round began, Kawika advanced quickly. Breathing hard as he backed away, Paul tried to slow him with a few jabs, but with his right arm lowered to protect his injury, he couldn't get enough speed on the punches. Sensing the weakness, Kawika pushed forward with reckless aggression, took a solid punch from Paul to the face, then fired two of his own—a jab to Paul's chest, an uppercut to Paul's chin. The second blow sent Paul stumbling backward for a few off-balance steps before he fell to the mat. As the referee began the count, Paul raised himself up on one knee and pressed his eyes closed against the glare of the overhead lights. When the referee reached eight he climbed back to his feet.

The fight resumed, and mere seconds passed before Kawika snapped Paul's head back with another right. Blood began to flow freely from Paul's nose, and when he brushed at it with his glove, he managed only to smear it across his face. Sensing the end, Kawika relentlessly pressed forward, his left glove straight out and shoved up against Paul's face to blind him, his right circling around whenever he had an angle. Most of the punches glanced off Paul's raised gloves or missed completely, but several caught Paul squarely in the face. In obvious pain, Paul lowered his head and shoved Kawika back with both gloves and then backpedaled away, wiping his face, his left eye swelling now and his nose still bleeding.

He tried to keep Kawika back with more left jabs, but Kawika, fueled by the drunken jeering, seemed to have lost his patience for measured attacks; he rushed forward, using his body like a plow to shove Paul back against the ropes. Cringing blindly, Paul ducked his head behind his gloves and tried to dodge to the side, but Kawika was already over him. Several blows slammed Paul's own gloves back into his face, others slapped against his stomach and body. Helpless, Paul rolled from side to side against the ropes, his head still lowered, his face still flinched. The shouts from the crowd increased in volume and emotion as another blow cut between Paul's gloves. Standing off to one side, the fat referee urged Kawika on.

Paul thrashed out blindly, trying to push away from the ropes, grunting with exertion and pain, when suddenly all the noise—all the clapping and screaming and drunken cheering—it all hushed into almost complete silence. It was as though all sound had suddenly drained from the world.

Bleeding from his lip and nose, one eye swollen and red, Paul looked over his gloves, watched as Kawika, staring out of the ring, stepped back and lowered his arms until they hung limp at his sides. The referee stood at the center of the ring as though he'd forgotten how to move or speak. Then Paul heard the shouting, a young voice that cracked:

"Stop it! Stop!"

It sounded like Lou's voice. Panting for air, Paul dropped to his knees and turned to look. A boy was sprinting from the trees across the dark field, past the broken-down pickup. Paul leaned over the middle rope, wiped the back of his glove over his eyes, looked again, his head lolling slightly on his neck as though he were drunk. The boy sprinted into the light without slowing. It was Lou. He climbed into the ring and knelt beside his father, who slumped against the ropes and let his head fall forward.

"What the heck is goin on?" Sammy shouted, standing up at the timekeeper's table.

His hand on his father's shoulder, Lou craned around to face Sammy. "Somebody help him!"

The men in the bleachers all seemed to have lapsed into a stupor and they stood staring at Lou, motionless. Paul tried weakly to stand, but he had no sense of balance and fell back hard against the ropes.

"Lou," he rasped, his eyes not quite focused. Across the ring from them, Jason hurriedly climbed through the ropes, followed by Carlos. Lou looked at the two men, then leaned over his father.

"You did good," he said, his voice strained. He tried to wipe some of the blood from Paul's face. "You did real good."

Crouching down, Jason took Lou by the shoulder and pulled him gently back, while Carlos threw his tackle box of medical supplies down on the mat and struggled to help Paul lift himself from the ropes. His face was bleeding badly, his body limp and heavy.

"Help me get him out of here," Carlos said to Jason.

They held Paul beneath the arms and helped him out of the ring. Sammy walked over to Carlos and in a voice soft enough that only he and Jason could hear said, "I want Coldwell and his boy gone before they ruin my tournament."

Carlos looked hard at Sam—just long enough to show his dislike for the man—and then he and Jason helped Paul past the beer-vending table and around the side of the restaurant. Lou followed closely behind his father, carrying Carlos's tackle box, wiping the angry tears from his face quickly so that perhaps no one would notice.

When they'd turned the corner, Jason could hear the men in the bleachers begin talking again, a quiet murmur like the sound heard in crowded theaters before the show begins. Not more than a few seconds later, as Jason and Carlos were helping Paul down onto a bench in front of the restaurant, Sammy's voice came over P.A. system:

"If that isn't the craziest ending ever to a fight I don't know what is! And just think, we still got three to go . . ."

CHAPTER 18

*A*lison was vacuuming around her tables when she heard the pounding at the door. For a startled moment she thought someone was trying to break into the restaurant, but then she saw it was Jason.

"What're you doing?" she asked, opening the door, annoyed that he had scared her. But then she saw Paul lying on his back on the outside bench, a young boy holding his hand, another man swabbing the blood from his face and trying to close the cut over his eye.

"Do you have your car here?" Jason asked, his voice full of urgency.

"What happened to him?"

"The tournament. Do you have your car?"

"I walked."

"Okay, I'm going home for my mom's car. Can you help until I get back? He's a friend of mine."

"Of course," said Alison, still trying to make sense of it all.

"I'll be back in a few minutes, Lou," said Jason, turning to the boy. "Alison's my girlfriend . . . I mean my friend . . . a good friend. She'll watch out for you until I get back."

Lou looked up at her through red eyes, nodded, and turned back to his father.

"Is he going to be okay?" Alison asked, whispering now.

"I don't know," whispered Jason. "There's more to it than just the fight."

"What's going on, Jas?"

"Just help them until I get back."

Jason turned away and set off at a jog through the dark parking lot.

"Jason?"

"This means more to me than you know, Alison," he called over his shoulder.

Alison looked after him for a moment; then she turned to the man closing the cuts.

"What can I do?"

CHAPTER 19

*P*aul sat slumped on a bench opposite his son in the back corner of Fat Sammy's, staring out of the booth at the empty restaurant. At the bar the overhead lights were turned off and the stools, upside-down on the counters, were silhouetted by the hazy neon signs in the window.

Alison came out from the workstation with two waters and set them on their table.

"Carlos said you should drink as much as you can."

Paul nodded. "You got any aspirin?" he rasped. "Carlos didn't have any."

"I'll go check."

She hurried back into the kitchen, leaving Paul alone with his son. For what seemed a long time, Paul sat staring at his water glass, tracing the edges of the tape on his eyebrow with a forefinger. His lower lip was swollen and cut, and his left eye half-closed. His boxing gloves and padded helmet lay on the table like a centerpiece. It was quiet.

His head ached and his ribs hurt when he breathed, but it was the shame that pained him most. The shame of taking such a beating in front of his son. The shame of letting the prize money slip away—money that could've put him that much closer to the twenty-thousand he'd promised to Teresa, to make sure she could provide well for Lou. He'd planned to give ten thousand to her for an emergency fund, and leave another ten thousand in a trust account for Lou. Teresa meant well and, he believed, really did want to help her son, but she had her own demons to battle. Paul had hoped that if he failed to help her conquer those demons in time, the money would help provide for Lou's well being, at least until he was eighteen. He knew he always had the foster care system to fall back on, but he didn't want Lou to have to suffer through that.

Lou picked up his fork and began tapping the edge of the table. Paul's eyes rose to meet Lou's. Lou put the fork down.

As of now he had only about seven thousand dollars in the bank, and a thousand of that had come from the sale of his truck. The amount grew steadily with each paycheck, but the headaches were getting worse, and occasionally his thoughts jumbled and he would find himself wondering why he'd just walked into the kitchen, or what he'd meant to get from the supply room at work. It was obvious now: there simply wasn't enough time.

"Maybe Melvin had me pegged all along," he said, voice barely audible, his cut lips pulling into a grim smile.

"Let's just forget tonight," Lou said. "He got one lucky punch."

Paul coughed and winced.

"Forget about tonight. Then what? Forget about last year? The year before that? Maybe the last fifteen years too—they haven't gone so good. Matter of fact, maybe I should just forget about my whole life."

"It don't matter," said Lou, staring back at Paul. "Whatever Melvin said, it don't matter."

Paul offered the same bleak smile. "It matters if he's right."

"Who cares what he said?" Lou's voice was loud, full of emotion. "You're my dad. I don't care."

Paul sighed deeply and let his head fall back against the bench. His eyes focused on the ceiling.

"You deserve better, Lou."

"Don't say this, Dad. Please don't say this."

Paul sighed deeply and closed his eyes. A tiny trickle of blood slipped out from beneath the tape over his eye and he wiped it away with the back of his hand. He spoke as though completely exhausted: "I should've told you this months ago. I'm sorry." He opened his red eyes. "I'm sick, Lou."

"No," Lou whispered. He was crying openly now, shaking his head. He wouldn't look at Paul.

"Listen to me, Lou! It's time to face facts."

"No . . ." Lou whispered. "No . . ."

"I'm dying, Lou. There's nothing anyone can do."

"No!" Lou screamed. He slid out from the table and broke for the door.

"Lou!" Paul yelled, rising from the bench. He tried to rush after him, but made it only a few steps before he felt as though a crack had opened in the front of his skull. The restaurant faded to shades of sepia and spun around him and he stumbled into another table, knocking the condiments to the floor. Broken angles of glass and splattered ketchup on the tile. The exit door swinging closed. Alison rushing from the kitchen.

And Lou was gone.

■ ■ ■

Jason and Paul sped through the quiet town in Nancy's Buick and turned onto Hollow Stone Drive. For nearly twenty minutes they'd been patrolling the dark streets, searching for the boy—until suddenly Jason realized where he'd gone, something he should've known from the beginning. Now, ahead in the soft gray moonlight, Paul could see the end of the road, the gate, and beyond and above that, the steep bluffs of the canyon. They stopped at Jason's house for a sledgehammer and then drove onto the dirt road and to the gate. Jason clicked on his high beams.

"How you know he's up there?" asked Paul.

"I just know," Jason said.

He got out and hit the padlock, once, twice with the sledgehammer. It broke with a dull clank. The hinges creaked dryly as Jason pushed the gate open, his shadow thrown up over the pale Russian olives by the headlights.

The Buick clunked over potholes and rocks, and reaching branches clicked against the windows and side panels. Paul looked out and watched the moon slide behind the passing trees. He wondered how Jason knew his son had come to this place, but his head ached and he felt too tired to ask.

When they arrived at Fire Creek, the headlights shone across the picnic area, lighting the broken tables and the shallow creek. The aspens at the edge of the clearing seemed almost to glow palely of their own accord and the leaves of the underbrush were sharp against deep black shadows. Away up in the pines, hardly more than a smudge of flickering light, Jason could see the orange glow of a fire. He stopped the car and set the park brake.

Without a word Paul got out and shut the door and limped slowly up, away through the trees toward the fire. Jason watched him receding into the shadows until he disappeared entirely. Then Jason turned off the engine and the headlights and sat on the hood to wait.

The moon moved slowly through the thin clouds, its gray light settling over the high broken ridges. The aspens whispered in the cool wind. The orange flicker of the fire ebbed until the darkness of the hill swallowed it entirely. Jason couldn't be sure how much time had passed—an hour, maybe two—before he heard them descending again. He got into the car, started the engine, turned on the headlights.

Paul and Lou were walking from the trees at the far end of the clearing. Paul rested a hand on Lou's shoulder, and the two of them moved with slow heavy steps, the boy struggling beneath his father's weight. Jason ran up to meet them and took Paul by the other arm. They exchanged no words, but Jason could see in their eyes, in their faces, that they'd shed tears together. But he guessed also by the way Lou struggled proudly to bear up his father's weight and help him back to the car that they'd come to some sort of understanding.

As for what was said, Jason didn't ask. He knew it was not his place to know. Silent, he helped them into the backseat, where Paul slouched back with his eyes barely open, his arm tightly around Lou's shoulder, Lou himself pressed up against his father as though he were a very young boy again.

As they drove slowly back down the canyon road, the moon disappeared into a thicket of darker clouds and everything faded to black; the canyon walls, the creek, everything shrank away into darkness, except for the hard dirt road and the trees to the side, still lit starkly by the headlights. In the low distance ahead, a few of the lights of Esperanza were shining, and above the valley, through the breaks between clouds, a few pale stars glimmered. The two fields of lights— sky and valley—seemed in that moment almost to be reflections of one another, as though there were no difference between them. But then the moon emerged again, and its gray light shone on the mountains and in the valley they saw dimly the streets, trees, and houses.

When they arrived back on Hollow Stone Drive, the porch light was on at Jason's house. He pulled the car into the carport. The garage door opened and Nancy, still dressed, stepped out. Jason had told her about Melvin and Teresa when he came home for the car, then phoned her from the restaurant about Lou. As Jason spoke to her now, explaining that everyone was okay, she came down the porch stairs and looked closely at Paul's bruised face and then gave him a quick tight hug. As though embarrassed, she pushed away quickly and then hugged Lou. They went inside, both families together, and Jason shut the door behind them.

CHAPTER 20

*J*ason eased Paul onto the guest bed and Nancy covered him with a thick quilt. His face had continued to swell, and now he couldn't see through his left eye and his cheeks and forehead were red and raw. It was difficult to tell whether he was awake or asleep.

"He's going to be okay, right?" Lou asked, looking at his father, at Jason and Nancy.

Nancy hadn't taken her eyes off Paul's face. If it was possible, he looked even worse now in the light of the bedroom lamp than he had in the carport. "We may need to take him to the hospital," she said quietly.

"No!" Paul said at once, struggling to raise his head and look at them. "No hospitals."

"It's okay, Paul," said Jason. "I can drive you. Lou can stay here while we're gone."

"Please," said Paul. He'd now given up trying to sit and lay there breathing hard, one eye open. "No."

"You need help, Dad," said Lou.

"I . . . don't have . . . insurance."

Jason and Nancy exchanged a look, neither sure what to do now.

"Does he mean money?" asked Lou.

No one answered.

"If it's money, you can use the savings account . . ."

"You don't understand . . . that money's not for me . . . Jason, tell him he doesn't understand . . ."

Jason put his hand on Lou's shoulder to reassure him.

"If he gets worse tonight," he said, as evenly as he could, "I promise we'll go straight to the hospital."

Hearing this, Paul seemed to relax: his breathing grew less ragged and labored and he slipped his arms under the blanket as though to sleep. They stood over the bed, watching him.

"Read to me, Lou," Paul said, his voice nothing more than a whisper now.

"Now?" asked Lou.

"Please."

"What does he mean?" Jason asked.

"The Bible," Lou said. "When his headaches get real bad he sometimes asks me to read to him. He says it calms him down."

Nancy opened a drawer and took a set of scriptures and passed them to Lou, who opened them and searched for a place to read.

"We should go now," Nancy whispered to Jason.

Jason nodded.

"We're right out here if you need anything," he said.

As they slipped out and shut the door, they heard Lou beginning to read the Psalms of David.

■ ■ ■

"So what now?" Nancy asked. They were sitting at the kitchen table, drinking an herbal tea Nancy had just poured from the kettle.

"He'll have to stay . . . at least until he feels better."

"And if he doesn't ever feel better?"

"Where else can he go?"

Nancy nodded and sipped her tea.

"Tomorrow I'll call my old friend Greg Martin in Salt Lake," she said. "His wife's an oncologist. Maybe we can get Paul in to see her."

They sat for a while, listening as every now and then a fragment of Lou's reading came loud enough into the kitchen that they could make out the words.

"It's funny," said Jason, "but a week ago I thought I had this all figured out."

"What?"

"Why God saved me. I thought maybe he wanted me to help Lou and Paul. But nothing I've done makes any difference . . ."

"That's not true at all."

Jason looked up at her.

"And besides, we don't know how this story ends yet, Jason. Don't give up hope."

Nancy squeezed his shoulder gently and then stood.

"I'm going to go get a bed set up for Lou."

She kissed Jason on the forehead and left him alone at the kitchen table, staring down at the steam rising from his mug.

CHAPTER 21

*F*ire Creek was quiet and still, the only noise the birds hidden high away in the trees. Before him stood Lou's fort, a ragged collection of oddly shaped lumber nailed along strange lines, somehow standing and managing to look vaguely like the structure Paul had built all those years ago. In front of it, the ashes from Lou's fire the night before lay black and cold within the circled rocks. There was something sad about it all, a sense of futility and naivete and loss.

Jason had come here looking for what?—answers? peace? escape?—he didn't know. Whatever his goal, what he'd found was anger. He thought about Rodney and his own father and Paul and Lou. Nothing turned out the way it was supposed to. If a stupid rock had been moved over a few inches, he would've known none of this. And then, almost as if hearing it again, the voice came back to him. *Don't stand up.*

"What do you want from me!" he screamed.

In the abrupt silence that followed even the birds went quiet. When no answer came, he picked up the hammer Lou had left beside the fort and smashed it through one of the haphazard walls. A few of the boards tore free and fell inward, and for a moment it seemed the whole unbalanced fort might follow. But somehow it held, and when Jason calmed enough to look at what he'd done, he found there on the floor a picture of a young boy staring back at him. It had been taped to the wall and fallen when the hammer struck.

He knew at once what it was—a picture of Paul as a boy standing in front of the old fort. He was smiling and proud and happy. Jason picked up the picture and looked at it, feeling the weight of so much time, change, tragedy start to suffocate him. But then in his mind he saw the dream again, his own father standing across the street, smiling at him, waiting for him, calming him. And he saw suddenly, as though the thought had been given to him, that there was no going back and no stopping from going forward and that in a sense this was exactly what he'd wanted to do all this time. But Lou knew this, just as he knew his father was sick, perhaps even dying. And still he built. Thinking of his own father, Jason felt now what it meant for Lou to build, though he couldn't have put this feeling into words. The answer, if a gesture of blind hope and compassion could be called such a thing, was here, at Fire Creek. Lou somehow understood.

Jason looked one last time at the picture. Then he slipped the top of it under a board nailed to the wall, where it could hang until Lou came back. But it wasn't enough. He had to build too. He took up the hammer again and scavenged for nails, and when he found them he put them to wood and continued the work Lou had already begun.

CHAPTER 22

*O*n Tuesday evening Paul felt well enough to return home, but Nancy wouldn't let him go without several boxes full of groceries. Soon after Jason had finished hauling it all over to the old house, Rooster showed up at the door, shaking a piece of lined paper filled with names and phone numbers in Jason's face.

"What is that?" asked Jason.

"A list of people around here who want to help."

"Help what?"

"Fix up Paul's house, bro."

"What're they going to do to it?"

"Watch for me tomorrow, dude," Rooster said, jumping down the porch steps and jogging away toward his house. "You'll get a feel for it then!"

The next morning, even though he was suffering through another headache and occasional bouts of dizziness, Paul insisted on going back to work. So Lou came over and he and Jason watched a movie. As it played they sat and talked about Teresa Roberts. Lou said he hadn't seen her in nearly four years, adding that Paul had recently begun speaking very highly of her whenever the opportunity arose, and sometimes even when it didn't. Lou figured if he had to move (he said nothing about Paul's condition) he'd much rather live with Teresa than Melvin.

When the movie finished, they went out to the front yard, and there they saw Rooster, four guys from the neighborhood, and two older men Jason knew by face only. They'd backed a truck up to the front door and were unloading rolls of carpet. Jason and Lou walked over to see what they were doing. Rooster and his crew had already finished the living room and were now laying the pad in the hall and two bedrooms.

"John Sorensen," one of the older men said, grabbing Jason's hand and shaking it. "I own Magic Carpets down on Third South. Rooster called me and told me what you two had goin on. Happy to pitch in."

"Who's paying for all this?" Jason asked.

"Bah," said Sorensen, waving a hand. "This is all just secondhand stuff and scraps. As long as he don't mind different colors in all the rooms it's no harm for me. In fact, I'll claim this as a charitable contribution on my taxes and probably pocket a few bucks."

He laughed, slapped Rooster on the back, and walked away to his truck to check a few measurements. Jason was still trying to make sense of how Rooster had managed all this when Alison appeared in the doorway, dressed in work clothes, a toolbelt around her hips.

"Oh, you're finally here," she said, smiling. "Rooster told me what you'd been up to all this time—I'm glad someone finally did—and I'm here to help. Come on and give me a hand."

Without another word she disappeared back into the house. Jason turned to Rooster for an explanation.

"Come on, man!" Rooster said, raising his hands in surrender. "It was a stroke of genius! Who else could get more work out of you than her?"

"I don't know if it's like that anymore."

"Please! I see the way you look at her." Rooster dropped to one knee, raised one hand in a pose stolen from some classical oratory, and in a deep wavering voice intoned, "But, soft! What light through yonder doorway breaks? It is the east and Alison is the—"

Jason grabbed him and tried to make him stand up again. "She's going to hear you!"

Lou, who had been silent to this point, decided to join the game: "Jason's in *love?* Can it be true?"

"You guys are pathetic," said Jason, but he was outnumbered and outwitted, so he shook his head in defeat and retreated into the house, trying his best to hide his smile.

He and Alison worked in the spare room, pulling out the old baseboards and broken tack strips to prepare for the new carpet, talking over the usual harmless subjects, catching up on all the insignificant details that friends know about one another. The work went slowly—too many breaks for talking and laughing and teasing— but neither seemed to mind.

Near the end of the job, Alison happened to look up and see the top shelf of the closet, which would normally be hidden by the header, but from where she worked on the floor she could just see an old shoebox. Carefully, she took it down and blew off years of dust. Across the lid in purple marker, following the slow lines of a child's script, the name *PAUL* had been written.

"What is it?" asked Jason.

"I don't know. Should I open it?"

"Might as well. If it's anything valuable we can give it to Lou to give to him."

Slowly, as though it were some precious relic, Alison opened the lid.

"Oh my goodness," she said putting a hand to her mouth. She passed the box to Jason. Inside, arranged in neat compartments which Paul had evidently glued together using pieces of other boxes, twelve homemade toy robots slept. Some had buttons for heads, others popsicle sticks for bodies and arms; one had a painted shield made from a can lid, another bat-like wings shaped from fabric and copper wire. Above each compartment Paul had written that robot's name.

Jason read the first few aloud: "Chomper. Lobsterbot. Scrap Head. Blast-o-matic." He paused, looked up at Alison. "These are amazing."

Alison carefully took one out of the box and turned it over in her hands, and as she looked at it something like sadness came over her.

"Are you all right?" Jason asked.

"How's Paul doing?" she asked, without looking up from the tiny robot.

Jason sighed and sat down against the wall. "Not good. His face is healing, but his headaches are getting worse. Sometimes he gets confused for no reason."

Alison turned the robot over once more, and then she suddenly put it back in the box and closed the lid. She sat down beside Jason but didn't look at him.

"Did you see people die in Afghanistan?"

"Yeah."

"People you knew?"

Jason nodded. They sat there, the box on the floor between them.

"Are you okay?" Jason asked, after a while.

"I've been waiting tables and studying botany."

"I don't understand."

"You've been at war, Paul's dying, and Lou's mother won't take him without twenty-thousand dollars tagging along. Meanwhile, I'm studying flowers and earning a few bucks, waiting for you to get over everything."

"You don't have to say this."

"Yes I do. And I can't see why any of this even matters if it can't keep Paul from dying."

"You don't want to think like that. Trust me. I know where it takes you."

"How else can I think about it?"

For a time, Jason said nothing. He sat wondering how best to answer the question, whether he would be a hypocrite if he said anything, whether he even now believed the words he had in mind. In the end, he chose to speak.

"I'm not sure, Alison, and I think I doubt it more than I believe it, but I've had these, I don't know what to call them—moments of clarity? Maybe that's not the right word . . . but at times I've *felt* this all matters exactly because of what it is right now, how it shapes us and changes us, who we become because of it. And when it's gone there'll be no going back, but that doesn't mean this moment didn't matter. Am I even making any sense?"

"I think so. But what about Lou? Will it still be worth it for him after his dad's gone?"

"I can't sit here and tell you what the answer is for him or anybody else. I think everyone has to decide that on their own. But as I see it there are only two real choices."

Alison looked at him, waited for him to continue.

"Despair or hope. I've had enough of the first one. And if that book you gave me really is true, then even God suffered, worse than any of us."

Alison sat thinking for a time; then she picked up the box, opened it once more, and looked over Paul's creations.

"They really are incredible, aren't they?"

"He must've been an amazing child."

Alison smiled sadly and closed the lid.

"You ready to finish this?" she asked.

"I hope so," Jason said.

■ ■ ■

Jason had worried that Paul might be angry, but Lou told him the next day that his father was deeply touched. So Rooster kept the crews coming. Over the next two weeks, a few of the neighborhood kids and their parents came and pulled weeds. Joseph McMurrin, an old farmer from the other side of town, drove over in this tractor and tilled the soil while his wife, Betty, planted grass and flowers. Two local carpenters fixed up the kitchen. Rooster's father showed up with a crew from Deseret Industries and brought in a few pieces of used, but salvageable bedroom and living room furniture. Jake Bryant and Dale Pinkart, two guys Jason had gone to high school with, painted the darkly stained walls of the house with a fresh coat of white. The wife of Greg Martin, Nancy's old friend, called back and arranged for Paul to drive out for a consultation. Every day, it seemed, Rooster had somebody or something lined up. Jason, Alison, and Lou worked with them daily, but at times Jason couldn't help but wonder what it all meant for Paul. And he worried a great deal for Lou.

Then a remarkable thing happened. Nancy came home from church the first week in September and said Paul and Lou had attended. Paul had stood and offered a tearful thanks to those who'd come to his house. He said it looked better than it had since his parents died, and this meant more to him than they could know. He concluded by saying he believed in God, always had in his own way, and he knew he might yet be healed. He asked for their prayers on behalf of his son and himself. He said he hadn't yet given up hope.

But the following morning, the oncologist called and said he'd reviewed Paul's tests. She was sorry to say she agreed with the original assessment: the tumor was inoperable. They could try chemotherapy, but it would be expensive, have serious side effects, and would most likely prove ineffective in Paul's case. Radiation therapy was out of the question due to the tumor's size and position. She prescribed stronger pain pills for the headaches and anti-nausea pills for the vomiting, and told Paul that most people in his shoes wouldn't make it to the new year. She did add, however, that there was always hope he might make it a little longer, since he'd come this far with only minor symptoms, relatively speaking.

When Paul hung up the phone, Lou didn't need to be told what had been said. He went to his father and they sat together in the remodeled kitchen and cried.

■ ■ ■

One cool morning in late September, when the red and yellow leaves flared on the hillsides, Jason came out to get the mail and found Paul standing in his yard, looking at his house. He and Rooster had recently put up new rain gutters, and for a moment Jason thought he was checking their work. But then he saw that Paul had no shoes on, was holding a spatula, and seemed to be talking to himself.

When Jason arrived at his side he knew at once that something was wrong. Paul's brow was furrowed and he was mumbling incoherently. He seemed startled when Jason asked him if everything was all right.

"Fine," he said, but his voice was a bit slow and slurred. "I'm just . . . I'm . . . Pancakes."

Ten minutes later, Jason, Lou, Paul, and Nancy sat in the Changs' kitchen. Paul had his head down, and the other three watched him intently. He said he felt fine now, that he'd just been a little confused and had had trouble getting the words out to explain himself. They ate dinner together and Paul and Lou went home.

The next morning, Lou was at the door at six a.m.

"My dad's really sick," he said, his face pale. "I need your help."

Paul spent the day locked away in the Changs' guest bedroom with the lights out and the blinds drawn. When he tried to speak, his voice again was slurred and he managed only to say that his head hurt fiercely before getting frustrated and refusing to speak anymore. Nancy called Doctor Hales, the local general practitioner, who prescribed even stronger pain and nausea medications, but said there was nothing more he could do.

Paul and Lou spent the night with the Changs, and when Paul didn't feel much better the next day, he stayed again. By the weekend, Jason and Lou had moved all of his clothes and personal belongings into the guest room, and without ever saying so aloud, they all knew he would be staying for the foreseeable future.

Nancy now brought much of her work home so that she could help Jason care for Paul. By the beginning of October, his headaches and nausea had quit entirely, but now he grew easily confused and forgetful, and more often than not his words were slurred, almost as though he were speaking with a grape under his tongue. Yet he insisted on going to church with Nancy each Sunday, and in the evening he called them together and asked them to read to him from the New Testament, claiming that somehow the words comforted him.

By this time, of course, Paul had been forced to "take a leave of absence" from his job, and on a Tuesday evening Boyd Grummet drove out to the house and spoke with Paul for a time. He wished him a get well on behalf of all his co-workers, and he apologized if he'd been hard on Paul.

"I had no idea you was goin through all this," he said sadly.

As he was about to leave, Jason had an idea. He walked with Boyd out to his car and they spoke for a time. When he came back into the house, he told Lou and Paul that Boyd was going to get them a key to the new lock on the gate, and that they were welcome to drive up to Fire Creek anytime they wanted to. He said if anyone gave them trouble to have them call up Boyd himself and he'd set them straight.

Often for the next few weeks, Paul, Lou, and Jason, and sometimes Alison and Nancy, would drive up the canyon and walk to the fort Lou had built (with a bit of help from Jason at the end). The wind was cold now, and the floor of the picnic area was littered with the yellow leaves of the now-bare aspens. Though the fort was not what Paul's had once been—the walls were crooked and misaligned, there was no door, the roof no longer had any shingles—it was wonderful all the same. Every time Paul saw it, he praised Lou for his craftsmanship, and when he was up to the task, he told stories about his childhood and his parents and the things they'd done at Fire Creek. He pointed out the tree with the lovers' names and said that his father had carved it one day to make up with his mother after a fight. He talked about how he and his friends had camped there and made big plans for the rest of their lives and had kept a stash of candy and beef jerky in a strongbox hidden under a rock nearby. He also told his son how Lou's grandmother and grandfather had been religious people in their own way, and that he was deeply sorry he'd allowed that to slip out of their lives for so long. Sometimes, for hours at a time, Paul would merely sit on one of the old chairs Jason and Lou had hauled up to the fort, a thick blanket over his legs, watching the wind high in the trees and the heavy autumn clouds and the geese moving slowly across the sky.

Over those weeks, Jason grew very close to Paul and Lou. They spent most of their days together, and in the afternoons when Paul slept, Jason and Lou often walked the hills and talked. And though their friendship grew, so did Jason's despair. He knew that soon it would end and Lou and Paul would be gone and he would be left to make sense of it all. Often these thoughts felt too heavy to bear.

In late October, at Paul's request, Jason called Teresa Roberts to check up on her. Paul would've called himself, but he had trouble now holding long conversations and he could be difficult to understand. As Teresa spoke, Jason had a sense that something was wrong—something in the quiet reluctance with which Teresa answered each question. At the end of the conversation, Teresa broke down in tears, explained through her sobs that she'd lost her job and was being evicted. She had no choice but to move in with an old boyfriend. When Jason asked if she was drinking or shooting up again, she sniffled and cried and refused to answer.

That evening, Nancy called her brother Marty, a social worker in Salt Lake City. By the next weekend he'd sent over all the paperwork they needed—government forms for Paul, Teresa, and Nancy to sign and notarize. Over dinner, Nancy and Jason explained their options: Lou didn't have to move in with Teresa—in fact, given recent changes, that now seemed impossible. Her voice calm and sincere, Jason told them they could make arrangements such that, if they wanted, Lou could remain with the Changs in Esperanza if things went badly for Paul. For a time, Paul stared down at his food. Lou watched him intently and waited. Just as Jason was beginning to wonder if perhaps he'd not understood, Paul began to weep. He rose from the table and took Lou by the hand and led him out of the room, leaving Jason and Nancy alone at the dinner table. A short time later, they returned, and Lou, also crying now, rushed across the room to hug Nancy. He shook Jason's hand first, but then they too embraced. Paul watched from the doorway. The decision had been made.

With Marty's help, the arrangements were finalized by the beginning of November. That same week, Paul, whose condition continued to decline, asked Jason one day at Fire Creek if he would come with them to church. The simple question took Paul nearly a full minute to ask, and Jason knew he couldn't refuse. So on the first Sunday in November, Jason dusted off his suit and tie and accompanied his mother, Lou, and Paul to the church.

The meeting passed without incident, and as far as Jason could tell Paul spent the time sleeping. The conclusion, however, must've been arranged beforehand without Jason's knowledge, because with ten minutes left in the hour, Paul rose from the bench and walked slowly to the pulpit. Knowing that he often had difficulty now speaking even simple sentences, Jason thought that he should go after him and bring him back to the bench, but Nancy put her hand firmly on Jason's leg and told him to wait.

Paul stood at the pulpit and looked over the congregation for nearly a minute before speaking. And then, in a moment of rare lucidity, he began to tell them about his childhood in Esperanza. He told them about his parents, the good people that they were, the good home they'd provided for him. He paused again, then said with only a slight slur, "December 16, 1984."

He looked over the congregation once more and continued, "Some of you still remember that date . . . the day of the explosion . . . the Esper . . . at the Esper . . . at the warehouse. My parents . . . I lost them both in the explosion. Daddy worked in the warehouse and forgot his . . . forgot his lunch. He forgot his lunch and Mommy . . . she wanted . . . she took it to him." He paused, and a tear slid down his cheek. "For a long time . . . I was very bitter. I was so very bitter. I left my parents' faith, left God . . .

"I've seen the way you all have tried . . . you have helped me with my house. It hurt me to live there knowing . . . knowing what it was before . . . but now it's nearly back. Thank you.

"But there are things . . . some things are more important. When I found out I was sick, I turned back to God . . . turning back because I was desperate . . . but I didn't love him. I am touched by your kindness . . . I am praying still . . . I feel God's arms around me . . ."

Paul paused, looked directly down at Jason, Lou, and Nancy. "I am a dying . . . I am going to die soon. My time . . . nearly at an end, but I'm not . . . I feel not afraid. My son, I now know this . . . he will be taken care of. I am praying now . . . praying every day, every day, he won't have the same bitterness." Paul seemed to be looking directly at Jason. "I am at peace . . . and I think . . . in the end our wounds are going to be healed . . . No more scars . . . No more scars or wounds . . . No more scars or wounds." Paul sighed, wiped his eyes. He turned away from the podium and walked slowly back to the bench.

He never spoke so effortlessly again. He spent most of his days in bed, and when he tried to rise he had trouble with his balance and eyesight. Those were long days, and Lou spent them with his father in the Changs' guest room, reading episodes from the New Testament, over and over again. Two weeks later, early on a mid-November morning, as the sun rose over the frozen valley, Paul stopped breathing.

CHAPTER 23

*O*utside the Changs' home snow fell from a gray morning sky, and Hollow Stone Drive was white and quiet. To the east clouds draped themselves across Fire Creek Canyon. It was Christmas morning.

In the Changs' living room lights blinked from the branches of the tree. Beneath it, presents of many colors and sizes, and on the mantel, three stockings. The first to wake, Jason was sitting on the couch, looking at the pictures Nancy had tacked side-by-side to the wall near the tree. The first was of Jason's father and mother, in their mid-twenties, smiling in wedding formal wear. The second was Jason's portrait from his senior year in high school. The third was the picture that had hung in the Coldwells' entryway, the one in which Paul, seated beside Lou, smiles awkwardly and tries to cover the hole in his jeans.

Jason looked for a time at the third picture, then settled back on the couch and closed his eyes. He knew the others would be waking soon, but for now he was glad to be alone, to listen to the falling snow tapping quietly at the window.

A half hour later Jason heard Nancy walk out to the kitchen, where she began making Christmas breakfast. Soon Jason could smell and hear the bacon and eggs sizzling in the pan, could hear Nancy humming Christmas hymns. She didn't know Jason was awake, and he preferred it this way. He sat up quietly and looked out the window into the vague gray light. The flakes, wide and slow, spun past the window. Across the street, the Coldwells' house was dark, dusted with snow. A "For Sale" sign hung from a post at the curb, but Jason knew it would probably sit vacant for a long time. When the copper markets dipped over a decade earlier, lay-offs followed, and scores of houses just like the Coldwells now sat vacant across the valley. But whether the house sold or not made no real difference anymore.

Jason closed his eyes again and for a time drifted into a dreamless sleep.

When he awoke, Lou was awake. Jason could hear him in the kitchen with Nancy, helping prepare the breakfast. They were cutting fruit and mixing a pitcher of juice. Jason rose and stood before the window. The snow had quit, and away to the east the morning sun was breaking through the gray clouds, its light brilliant and glaring on the white hills above Fire Creek. Jason knew from his conversation with Boyd Grummet the previous week, when he visited him to return the key, that in the spring Fire Creek would be leveled to make way for a construction staging area: the plans to open the new mine were finally moving forward.

Jason looked at the canyon. The rebuilt fort would soon be destroyed; Fire Creek would be bulldozed; the Coldwell house would be sold eventually at a low price to buyers unaware of its history, or, more likely, it would sit vacant, slowly gathering back the dust and decay of years. Jason thought of the good people who had gone from his life—his father, Rodney, and now Paul; and he thought that someday his mother also would pass on, as would he, as would Lou, and this house they now shared would one day crumble and the mine would yield its last load of copper and the town would be slowly claimed once more by the wilderness from which it had been born.

In the kitchen Lou laughed and Nancy told him to go wake up lazy Jason.

"I'm already up," Jason called.

Nancy and Lou came into the living room. Nancy wore her stained, rust orange apron, Lou his sweats and a tank top and a pair of new wire-rim glasses. Jason smiled at them. "Been up for a while," he said. "Just enjoying the scenery."

Nancy and Lou understood. Over the last few weeks they'd each needed their own time, their own space. But now it was Christmas morning, and Nancy said that breakfast was ready, and the three of them walked together to the kitchen and sat at the table, where Nancy's best china had already been set. They prayed over the food, but before they ate, Nancy announced she had a special present for Lou that he should open first. She took a small wrapped box from one of the cupboards and set it on the table before Lou.

"From you?" he asked, shaking the package.

"Read the card," said Nancy.

As Lou opened the envelope taped to the box, Jason leaned over and at the bottom saw Paul's name. When Lou finished the card, he looked up, his eyes soft, his smile somewhat saddened, and waited for an explanation.

"He asked me to get it for you two months ago. He'd hoped to be here to give it to you today, but . . ."

Nancy didn't finish the thought. She couldn't. Carefully, Lou pulled off the wrapping paper and opened the box. Inside, a handsome leather-bound Bible. In gold cursive across the bottom of the cover: Lou Gene Coldwell.

"Open it," said Nancy.

Lou turned to the first page, and there he found Paul's slow script carefully observing the margins. For a time Lou read quietly; Jason watched him, but he couldn't quite make out the words from his place at the table, nor did he try. Lou laughed, perhaps a bit sadly, at something he read, then he laughed again. When he finished he carefully shut the cover and set the book aside on the counter, away from the meal.

They ate quietly, and as they finished their food, snow began falling again. Jason could see it out the kitchen window, large lazy flakes that filled the still air. Four children in bright winter clothes and heavy boots tromped up the sidewalk past the window, hauling shiny new sleds to the hills at the end of the street. A moment later, Rooster followed, panting, calling to them to wait. He paused, leaning on his knees, to catch his breath and saw Jason, Lou, and Nancy inside. Laughing, he packed a snowball lightly and thudded it against the window.

"I'll take you guys down later!" he yelled, his voice quiet behind the glass. He laughed again, struck a few bodybuilder poses, and ran off after his siblings.

Jason could still hear them shouting, calling to one another to race. And then they were too far away and the neighborhood was again quiet, still.

When they finished breakfast, they cleared the dishes. Nancy knew that Alison was coming over later that morning, and she asked if Jason wanted to wait to open presents. But before he could answer, Lou informed them both that there would be no waiting—not even for Alison. So Nancy, laughing, explained that either way they still had to observe first the Chang family tradition of reading from St. Luke. They took their Bibles into the living room and sat beside the tree, where Nancy asked Lou if he would be their narrator and put his father's present to good use.

As Lou peeled open his fresh pages, Jason looked once more out the window and watched the snow falling slowly, quietly over Esperanza. The world was peaceful, calm, white. Once more he thought of his father, whom he never knew, he thought of Rodney and Erika and their daughters, and he thought of Paul. He saw the "For Sale" across the street and he thought once more of Fire Creek, soon to be leveled. Lou had found the page now, and he began reading: "And it came to pass in those days, that there went out a decree from Caesar Augustus, that all the world should be taxed . . ."

Jason listened, and he knew that all stories must end. All things must fade. He watched the snow falling over Hollow Stone Drive, the lights blinking in the tree, and Lou reading from his new scriptures. He looked at the pictures of Paul, of his father, and the pain of losing them rose up in his chest.

"Fear not," Lou was reading. "For, behold, I bring you good tidings of great joy, which shall be to all people . . ."

Jason missed Rodney. He missed Paul. He wished he could've known his father. He wondered why Paul's father had to forget his lunch that day nearly twenty years earlier, why his mom decided to take it to him at 11:30, why his own father decided to run inventory that day. But the world outside was beautiful, white, and new, and all things in this world must change.

And so Jason listened to Lou read and looked at the photos on the wall and let himself imagine what his own father might say to him, years from today, when they would embrace for the first time and sit down to speak.

LIFESONG-BYU BRANDED BOOKS BY PALMYRA PRESS

Palmyra Press is proud to present books by writers from Brigham Young University's Lifesong program. Lifesong Stories and Films is an institute at BYU where writers and filmmakers collaborate to create high-quality, challenging, and ultimately faithful novels and films. The institute adheres to a tradition of telling stories through compact, highly visual scenes that engage readers and viewers. The results are dynamic, fast-paced stories that invite readers to think deeply about the roles family and spirituality play in their lives.

To learn more about Palmyra Press, contact us:

Palmyra Press
362 N. Bedford Street
E. Bridgewater, MA 02333
www.palmyrapress.com